B
R
Wren, Laura Lee
Christopher Reeve
Hollywood's Man of Courage

# Christopher Reeve

# The People to Know Series

**Neil Armstrong**
*The First Man
on the Moon*
0-89490-828-6

**Isaac Asimov**
*Master of Science Fiction*
0-7660-1031-7

**Willa Cather**
*Writer of the Prairie*
0-89490-980-0

**Bill Clinton**
*United States President*
0-89490-437-X

**Hillary Rodham Clinton**
*Activist First Lady*
0-89490-583-X

**Bill Cosby**
*Actor and Comedian*
0-89490-548-1

**Walt Disney**
*Creator of Mickey Mouse*
0-89490-694-1

**Bob Dole**
*Legendary Senator*
0-89490-825-1

**Marian Wright Edelman**
*Fighting for
Children's Rights*
0-89490-623-2

**Bill Gates**
*Billionaire
Computer Genius*
0-89490-824-3

**Jane Goodall**
*Protector of
Chimpanzees*
0-89490-827-8

**Al Gore**
*United States
Vice President*
0-89490-496-5

**Tipper Gore**
*Activist, Author,
Photographer*
0-7660-1142-9

**Ernest Hemingway**
*Writer and Adventurer*
0-89490-979-7

**Ron Howard**
*Child Star &
Hollywood Director*
0-89490-981-9

**John F. Kennedy**
*President of the
New Frontier*
0-89490-693-3

**John Lennon**
*The Beatles
and Beyond*
0-89490-702-6

**Maya Lin**
*Architect and Artist*
0-89490-499-X

**Jack London**
*A Writer's
Adventurous Life*
0-7660-1144-5

**Barbara McClintock**
*Nobel Prize
Geneticist*
0-89490-983-5

**Christopher Reeve**
*Hollywood's Man
of Courage*
0-7660-1149-6

**Ann Richards**
*Politician, Feminist,
Survivor*
0-89490-497-3

**Sally Ride**
*First American Woman
in Space*
0-89490-829-4

**Will Rogers**
*Cowboy Philosopher*
0-89490-695-X

**Franklin D. Roosevelt**
*The Four-Term
President*
0-89490-696-8

**Steven Spielberg**
*Hollywood
Filmmaker*
0-89490-697-6

**Martha Stewart**
*Successful
Businesswoman*
0-89490-984-3

**Amy Tan**
*Author of
The Joy Luck Club*
0-89490-699-2

**Alice Walker**
*Author of
The Color Purple*
0-89490-620-8

**Simon Wiesenthal**
*Tracking Down
Nazi Criminals*
0-89490-830-8

**Frank Lloyd Wright**
*Visionary Architect*
0-7660-1032-5

People to Know

# Christopher Reeve
## *Hollywood's Man of Courage*

Laura Lee Wren

**Enslow Publishers, Inc.**

40 Industrial Road        PO Box 38
Box 398                Aldershot
Berkeley Heights, NJ 07922   Hants GU12 6BP
USA                               UK

http://www.enslow.com

**Library of Congress Cataloging-in-Publication Data**

Wren, Laura Lee.
    Christopher Reeve : Hollywood's man of courage / Laura Lee Wren.
        p.  cm. — (People to know)
    Includes bibliographical references and index.
    Summary: A biography of the actor famous for playing Superman, discussing his
activities before and after the accident that paralyzed him and focusing on his
determination to go on with his life despite his problems.
    ISBN 0-7660-1149-6
    1. Reeve, Christopher, 1952–    . —Juvenile literature. 2. Actors—United
States—Biography—Juvenile literature. 3. Quadriplegics—United States—
Biography—Juvenile literature. [1. Reeve, Christopher, 1952–    . 2. Actors and
actresses. 3. Quadriplegics. 4. Physically handicapped.] I. Series.
PN2287.R292W76    1999
791.43'028'092—dc21
[B]                                                                    98-29493
                                                                         CIP
                                                                          AC

Printed in the United States of America

10 9 8 7 6 5 4 3 2

**To Our Readers:**
All Internet addresses in this book were active and appropriate when we went to press.
Any comments or suggestions can be sent by e-mail to Comments@enslow.com or to
the address on the back cover.

# Contents

# Up, Up and Away!

It was 1976 and twenty-four-year-old Christopher Reeve was down on his luck. Thoughts of failure ran through his head. He had enjoyed his recent acting role on Broadway, but his reviews had not been favorable. He had given up that paying job to try for a starring role in a TV miniseries but was turned down. After spending much of his life onstage, Reeve was beginning to doubt his own talent.[1]

"I absolutely wrote myself off," Reeve remembered. "I was sponging off friends, sleeping on couches, turning into a vegetable until one day I said, 'This isn't right.'"[2]

Reeve's favorite escape was piloting his own plane. He would hop into the small aircraft, comforted by the roar of the engine. After an okay from the tower, he would increase his speed, climbing higher and higher into the air. He spent a lot of time in the wide expanse of the sky, flying his Cherokee 140 all over the country and trying to decide what to do with his life. When his agent would try to find him, he would be gone. "I parked in grass fields every night and camped out with a sleeping bag," Reeve said.[3]

With help from his father and his agent, Reeve was able to fight off his depression.[4] In January 1977, Reeve was in a New York City casting office when he got a phone call that would soon change his life.

Meanwhile, young movie producer Ilya Salkind was also in trouble. He and his partner—his father, Alexander Salkind—had been offered $25 million from Warner Brothers for their next film project about Superman, the comic book character with two identities, one "faster than a speeding bullet." They developed the script and hired Richard Donner as director. All they needed was a star.

The Salkinds thought finding the right actor would be easy. They were sure that Robert Redford would be perfect for the part, but he turned them down.[5] Ilya Salkind then offered the part to Paul Newman, who refused. Their Hollywood search grew wider.

James Caan said he would not get into that "silly suit."[6] Clint Eastwood was too busy. The Salkinds dismissed others, such as Steve McQueen, Charles Bronson, Sylvester Stallone (later to star in *Rocky*), and Bruce Jenner (the star of the 1976 Olympics), as not being right for the part. Hundreds of unknown actors auditioned. Ilya Salkind's wife, the actress

Skye Aubrey, even had her dentist fly to London for a screen test.[7]

The other roles in the movie filled quickly. Marlon Brando signed on to play the small part of Superman's father. Gene Hackman took the part of Superman's adversary, Lex Luthor. Shooting was scheduled to begin shortly, and the Salkinds still had not found their star.

Ilya Salkind complained to his casting staff and yet again went through the photographs in the Screen Actors' Guild directory. This time he took a closer look at a photo of a handsome young man with a chiseled jawline and bright blue eyes.[8] Could they risk a starring role on an unknown actor with only a few acting credits to his name? Salkind thought it over and decided to take a chance. That unknown actor was Christopher Reeve.

When Reeve took the call requesting that he interview for the role of Superman, his first reaction to the idea was "Poor Hollywood. How sad. Why can't they come up with something new and exciting?"[9] He almost turned down the interview with Ilya Salkind and Richard Donner at the Sherry Netherland Hotel in New York City. Since it was on the way to the station where he had to catch his train home, he decided to give it a shot.[10]

A boyish-looking Reeve arrived at the meeting, knowing he was too thin to portray a muscle-bound character. "[I looked] like Jimmy Stewart standing sideways," Reeve admitted.[11] But when Donner asked him to put on a pair of horn-rimmed glasses, Reeve called on his acting experience. "I decided Superman

*Christopher Reeve as the bumbling newpaper reporter Clark Kent in the movie* Superman.

would represent the side of me that would be everything in life I'd like to be," Reeve later recalled. "And as Clark Kent I'd take all my insecurities and exaggerate them for comic effect."[12] As he slumped his shoulders and concentrated on projecting a curious but innocent attitude, the personality of Clark Kent emerged.

The Salkinds were convinced that Reeve was their Superman and immediately flew him to London for a screen test. When reading the script, Reeve was delighted to find that it was more than a mere comic-book plot. He said it was a story "with a captivating blend of humor and heroics."[13] He was determined to do well in the screen test. He practiced as Clark Kent in old suits and glasses and even worked out the necessary makeup for his change into Superman. Reeve's test was a success. With the two-year search finally over, Donner said, "If there's a God in heaven, he sent me Christopher Reeve."[14]

Later, Reeve reflected on winning the part of Superman. He felt an eerie connection between his own personality and that of the Superman/Clark Kent character. He could easily relate to Clark Kent's innocent and optimistic attitude, while also sharing Superman's belief in the good in people and, of course, his love of flying.[15]

Reeve worked hard to fit the heroic image of Superman. In later years, after soaring to stardom as Superman, he tried just as hard to rid himself of the cape and boots. He did not want to be known only as Superman. Reeve acted in many different roles, though he did return to the Superman character for several sequels. He also used his celebrity status to support a variety of causes, such as human rights and preserving the environment. Sometimes he dressed in his Superman costume to visit terminally ill children.

When appearing as the superhero, Reeve would remind people that Superman was merely his screen personality. He would point out that there are many real-life heroes, from schoolteachers to police officers: "The definition of hero . . . is courage without looking for a reward."[16] He said that a hero is a person doing "a courageous action without considering the consequences."[17]

In 1995, Reeve, age forty-two, was a successful actor. Though the public still viewed him as Superman, he had been able to challenge himself with many different roles that achieved critical acclaim. In between films and theatrical projects, Reeve enjoyed skiing, sailing, bicycling, and horseback riding. He excelled at many sports, often taking them to the competitive level.

On May 27, Reeve left his wife and young son at a hotel while he entered a riding competition in Virginia. He was to take his horse through an obstacle course with a series of jumps. They cleared the first two jumps easily, but as they approached the third jump, Reeve's horse suddenly stopped. Reeve was propelled forward and flew off the horse, landing headfirst.

Fans gasped in horror when they learned that the tragic accident had left Reeve paralyzed from the neck down, unable even to breathe on his own. Those who

When he was paralyzed from the neck down in a horseback riding accident, Christopher Reeve faced his greatest challenge.

loved him—his family, his close friends—were all powerless to help. Christopher Reeve now faced his greatest challenge.

Today, Reeve has moved forward from that tragedy. He has continued his life as an activist, raising millions of dollars for research on spinal cord injuries, and he is still involved in the film industry as a director, a producer, and an actor. He is a loving husband and a devoted father. Just as the accident changed him physically, Reeve's new life in a wheelchair has given him new insights. Today he realizes that a hero does not have to perform a big, courageous act. A hero does not have to be famous or seem "larger than life." A hero, he now says, is "an ordinary individual who finds the strength to persevere and endure in spite of overwhelming obstacles."[18] How did Christopher Reeve's life prepare him to become just such a hero?

# "Being Somebody Else"

$C$hristopher Reeve was born in New York City on September 25, 1952, to Barbara Pitney Lamb and Franklin d'Olier Reeve. One year later his brother, Benjamin, was born.

While Barbara cared for the two little boys, sometimes taking them for carriage rides through Central Park, Franklin kept busy trying to support his growing family. He attended classes at Columbia University and did research toward his master's degree in Russian. He also taught Slavic language classes in between waiting on tables and hauling freight as a longshoreman, helping to unload banana boats at night.

When Chris was almost four years old, his parents split in a bitter divorce. The two boys moved with their mother to Princeton, New Jersey, where she became a writer for a local newspaper, *Town Topics.*

The boys were able to spend time with both parents, but Barbara and Franklin refused to speak to each other. After visits, Franklin dropped the boys off at the edge of Barbara's property. Chris worried about whose side he should be on, as if he needed to choose between his parents. He resented being torn between the two, feeling like a pawn in a war game.[1] He decided early not to depend on them or on anyone else.

In 1959, Barbara married Tristam B. Johnson, an investment broker who had four children from a previous marriage. The couple soon added two more boys of their own to the family, Jeffrey and Kevin. Franklin Reeve also remarried and had three children—Mark, Brock, and Allison—with his second wife. Chris and Benjamin found themselves part of two separate families with many stepbrothers, stepsisters, half brothers, and a half sister. In this crowd, Chris searched for a place to belong. He became something of a loner, avoiding close relationships so he would not risk their coming apart.

Chris attended the exclusive Princeton Country Day School, in an environment many would consider privileged. Dressed in jacket and tie, he rode the bus with neighbor Mary Chapin Carpenter, the future country music star, down streets lined with stately, ivy-covered buildings. Lake Carnegie was nearby, where Chris played hockey in the winter, and where one summer he and his brother Benjamin decided to set their goldfish free.[2]

Chris took advantage of the many opportunities

open to him, exploring a wide range of interests. He was not allowed to watch much television or read comics, but he did learn to ski in the Pocono Mountains of Pennsylvania, took piano lessons, and tried fencing.

One day, a representative from the McCarter Theatre in Princeton came into Chris's fourth-grade class and asked if anyone could sing. Chris sang out, "Mi, mi, mi." He soon landed a part in Gilbert and Sullivan's operetta *Yeoman of the Guard*.[3] His teachers supported his extracurricular pursuits, letting him out of school as long as he made up his homework.[4] While his classmates were working on their assignments, Chris would look at his watch, gather up his books and papers, then leave school early to get to the theater.

Chris grew quickly, and by age thirteen he was already six feet two inches tall. He often had painful, swollen knees and was diagnosed with Osgood-Schlatter disease. For teenagers with this condition, the tendons and bones grow at different rates. During that time, Chris needed to avoid all sports. He also had asthma and many allergies and even came down with alopecia areata, a condition that once caused patches of his hair to fall out. He felt awkward, especially when it came to girls. Even as an older teenager, he remained unsure of himself and lacked self-confidence.

Chris threw himself into many other activities. He continued his interest in playing piano, and for his sixteenth birthday, he received a Steinway grand piano as a gift from his mother. He acted as assistant conductor of the school orchestra, sang in a madrigal group, and enjoyed playing goalie for a hockey team—usually excelling in each pursuit. He had a competitive spirit and especially responded when there was a challenge to meet. If someone told him to do twenty repetitions of a certain exercise, he would instead shoot for thirty to thirty-five, always pushing himself to the limit.

Chris subjected his friends and teammates to those same high standards. During visits with his father, who was then a professor at Yale University in New Haven, Connecticut, Chris learned to sail. He entered many exciting races and won most of them. Later, though, he admitted that he would "terrorize" his crew as he pushed them to do their best. "I was really aggressive, demanding, and critical of myself and other people," he said. "If I didn't win, it would set me back for days."[5]

Chris was happy playing sports, but the theater was becoming more and more his focus. He continued performing parts in school plays and at the McCarter Theatre. If he did not have an acting role, he would do anything to remain a part of the show. For one production, he might be in the orchestra pit playing piano; for another, he might be a member of the chorus. Chris had found a place where he felt at home. At the theater, he could be comfortable in another character's skin, dealing with fictional problems. "Being somebody else took me away from a lot of things I was not prepared to deal with," Reeve remembered.[6]

In 1968, fifteen-year-old Chris got a summer apprenticeship at the Williamstown Theatre Festival in the small New England community of Williamstown, Massachusetts. There, his love of the theater grew. As an apprentice, he worked as a stagehand, building sets and moving props around during performances. He sold tickets in the box office. Finally, he got a speaking part with two lines in *How to Succeed in Business Without Really Trying*. "The theater . . . felt like an extended family to me because I was sort of adopted by many of the actors in the company," Reeve remembered.[7]

When he turned sixteen, Chris joined the Actors' Equity Association. Membership in this organization was unusual for such a young actor. He also hired an agent. Before starting to act full-time, however, Chris wanted to complete his education. He sent out applications for admission to various colleges, including Yale and Cornell universities, and anxiously awaited their replies.

Chris received a rejection from Yale, where his father taught, but an acceptance letter soon followed from Cornell, located in Ithaca, New York. He was delighted. His parents were happy with his choice, too. "They wanted me to be isolated from New York, where I wouldn't be tempted to go into the city and get a job," Reeve explained. Until he earned his degree, he said, "they wanted me away from the pressures of the marketplace."[8]

Reeve's agent was just as enthusiastic. From his viewpoint, Cornell—just a few hours' drive away—was still close enough to New York City that auditions would be possible.

In the fall of 1970, Christopher Reeve left his home

in Princeton, New Jersey, for the gothic-revival buildings of Cornell. Near the campus is Cayuga Lake, surrounded by scenic pathways and old willow trees, where students often go to relax.

This was a time of unrest in America. President Nixon had just expanded the Vietnam War by authorizing the invasion of Cambodia. Many college students were opposed to this and protested on campus. Reeve attended a few of those rallies, but more often he kept busy with other pursuits, such as helping to establish a residence hall for actors at the college.

Reeve majored in English and also took classes in theater arts and music theory. True to his nature, he explored many other opportunities as well. He volunteered at WVBR radio, sang in the Sage Chapel choir, and joined the sailing and hockey teams.[9] Many college students often spend more time at other activities than they do in the classroom. Reeve was no different, often heading to the ski slopes in the winter snow. He once joked, "It could be said that in the years I spent at Cornell I majored in skiing."[10]

Reeve continued working as an actor. Luckily, his agent understood that a college education was his top priority. He set up auditions and meetings around classes. "Somehow, I managed to balance the academic and professional sides of my life," Reeve said.[11]

While at Cornell, Reeve acted in many college plays, including *The Good Woman of Szechuan*, *Waiting for Godot*, and *A Winter's Tale*.[12] He threw himself totally into theater activities and was always serious about his acting studies. One summer he had

*In 1970, Reeve began his freshman year at Cornell University.*

a contract with the San Diego Shakespeare Festival to perform at the Old Globe Theatre. Looking back, though, he admitted, "I was dreadful."[13]

After the summer season, he moved back to bustling New York City after arranging to attend the Juilliard School for his senior year of college. Cornell University agreed to give him credit for his work at Juilliard. At the Lincoln Center for the Performing Arts, with the Metropolitan Opera House and the New York State Theater sharing a large plaza, the Juilliard School is right in the center of the theater world. The modern five-story building holds classrooms for music, dance, and drama students.

Reeve studied under instructor John Houseman (*The Paper Chase*) and began a long friendship with fellow student Robin Williams (*Mrs. Doubtfire, Flubber*). They seem such opposites in personality, with Williams the nonstop comic and Reeve always serious, but the two actors got along very well. Reeve attributed their friendship to the fact that he did not try to match Williams's comic style when they were together. Reeve remained his quiet self, laughing at his friend's humor.

One class project was to present theater to inner-city children, sometimes in school basements with low ceilings. During one performance in the Bronx, when Reeve was supposed to draw a sword and then flourish it, he accidentally knocked out the lights above him. "Glass flew everywhere, the lights went out, and the students roared their approval at this reckless destruction of school property," he said.[14]

While building friendships with fellow actors,

such as William Hurt (*Lost in Space, Michael*), Kevin Kline (*Dave, Silverado*), and Mandy Patinkin (*Chicago Hope, Yentl*), Reeve still had trouble playing the dating game. "I used to get bad attacks of cold feet. I found it difficult—and still would—to approach some girl who's . . . minding her own business," Reeve explained. "Making the opening line is like swimming across the Hudson River—you have to cross an incredible gulf."[15]

After earning his bachelor of arts degree in 1974, Reeve got a regular part on the TV soap opera *Love of Life.* He played the role of Ben Harper, who was not a very honorable character. "The guy had lots of money and no moral scruples whatsoever," Reeve said of his TV personality. "He was married to two women at the same time, one of whom was pregnant, and the Mafia had a contract out on him because of some blackmail-extortion scheme."[16]

Reeve learned then that many fans believe an actor truly is the character he plays. Once, a woman approached his table in a restaurant and hit him over the head with her purse. "How dare you treat your poor pregnant wife that way!" she shouted.[17] Reeve stuck with the unlikable character, and after two years on the soap he was able to repay his stepfather for his college education.

In between filming schedules, Reeve discovered another love: flying. In 1975, he took lessons in Princeton from instructor Robert Hall, who made sure Reeve took flying seriously. "He is one of the real tough, grouchy, chain-smoking, coffee-drinking, nail-biting instructors who is just worth his weight in gold," Reeve said of his instructor.[18] When Reeve moved back to New York City, he continued his lessons at Teterboro Flight Academy in northern New Jersey under instructor Lou Ranley. There Reeve completed the requirements for his pilot's license.

Reeve left the soap opera to make his Broadway debut in 1976, cast as Nicky in *A Matter of Gravity*. Reeve played the grandson of Katharine Hepburn, the legendary star he had watched on the movie screen since childhood.

Hepburn took a liking to the young actor and gave him acting tips, often while they were waiting in the wings to go onstage. Later, Reeve remembered his first Broadway experience: "She used to say to me, 'Now be fascinating, Christopher. . . .' I said, 'Well, that's easy for you to say. The rest of us have to work at it, you know.'"[19] Unfortunately, the play received poor reviews. Many critics raved about Hepburn's performance, but they were not impressed with the rest of the cast.[20]

Even though the show was not a Broadway success and closed after only a few months, Reeve gained much from the experience. "I'd always thought of acting as a way to lose yourself, disappear into a part, and thus find a kind of freedom," Reeve said. "[Hepburn] taught me that quite the opposite is supposed to happen. You must really bring your own convictions, things you really love and hate to the character, and adjust after that."[21] For years, Reeve and Hepburn kept in touch by writing letters.

Reeve's Broadway experience changed his relationship with his family. His parents had not spoken to

*Christopher Reeve on the television soap opera* Love of Life *with actress Birgitta Tolksdorf.*

*In 1976, Reeve made his Broadway debut in* A Matter of Gravity, *starring the legendary Katharine Hepburn (seated), who gave him some acting tips.*

each other in fifteen years. Instead of worrying about keeping them separated on opening night, Reeve said, "I . . . got my parents and stepparents tickets all together in the same row. They buried the hatchet."[22]

After his experience in *A Matter of Gravity*, Reeve was enticed by the prospect of making movies. With a Broadway credit under his belt, he was offered a small part in the movie *Gray Lady Down*, starring Charlton Heston. In this submarine adventure filmed in California, Reeve played an officer with very few lines. The movie received poor reviews and disappeared after a short run in the movie theaters in March 1978.

Then came a dry spell for Reeve. After working with such big stars as Hepburn and Heston, Reeve had hoped to be given a major part in the TV miniseries *The Captain and the Kings*. He was rejected. He had used his savings of about $8,000 from the soap opera job to buy a small plane, a Cherokee 140. He began spending a lot of time in the air or sitting in grassy fields, thinking about his past performances and the poor reviews. He was on the verge of depression.

Luckily, with encouraging words from his father and his agent, Reeve was able to shake his self-doubts. He later recalled that he simply decided it was time to stop flying off into the sunset. He returned to New York City, where he found a role in the theater production of *My Life*, starring his Juilliard classmate William Hurt. He was also chosen to be understudy in Broadway's *Dracula*. After only two rehearsals, however, he would turn in Dracula's black cape. Instead, Reeve would wear a red one, emblazoned with a supersized S.

# Superman

Reeve was not even thinking of his recent *Superman* audition when an announcement on the news show *Good Morning America* caught his attention. There on television was Rona Barrett, a Hollywood gossip reporter, stating that a new, young actor, Christopher Reeve, had been chosen for the part of Superman.[1] Was it true? Reeve's pulse quickened as he raced to the phone. After a few phone calls by his agent, the story was confirmed. Reeve was offered $250,000 for the role that would take a year and a half to film.

Reeve's luck had changed. After hearing he had the part, he called his mother. "This time I . . . land[ed] a big one—a tuna instead of a minnow."[2]

Professor Franklin Reeve ordered a champagne toast to celebrate. He told his son Christopher that the role of Jack Tanner was a great part. Then he asked who would play the part of Ann Whitfield, the female lead. Reeve suddenly realized that his father had misunderstood. Franklin Reeve thought his son was to be in *Man and Superman*, a classic play written by the famous British playwright George Bernard Shaw.[3] Reeve had to explain that it was the popular comic-book character he was to portray, opposite a character named Lois Lane.

The Superman of comic-book fame was created by a teenage boy, Jerry Siegel. In 1932, he had an idea for a comic-strip character from another planet who would come to Earth to defend freedom and justice. This hero would be almost invincible but would hide his secret identity by living a double life, appearing to be an average American citizen. "[He was] a character like Samson, Hercules and all the strong men I ever heard tell of rolled into one," explained Siegel.[4]

Another teenager, Siegel's friend Joe Shuster, drew the illustrations of the character, dressing him in a colorful cape and tights. This superhero soon became one of the most popular comic-book characters in the country.[5] The United States was just finding its way out of the Great Depression, a nearly decade-long period when thousands of factories closed, banks failed, and more than 10 million workers were unemployed. Youngsters flocked to drugstores for the latest comic books. They loved to read about the heroic deeds of the man with unique powers and his alter ego—newspaper reporter Clark Kent. During World

War II, Superman became their symbol of courage and determination, just as they believed that America was the preserver of moral values and democracy.[6]

In the 1950s, Superman became an extremely popular television series, starring actor George Reeves. It was a low-budget show. The actors always wore the same outfits so different episodes could be filmed at the same time without worrying about matching each character's clothing. Superman could crash through walls, and there were lots of explosions, but the most spectacular special effect was when Superman flew through the air. The same film sequence was used over and over. In one episode, when Superman flew in the opposite direction, the film had merely been turned over and the S on his uniform was backward!

The special effects used for the movie version would be much better. Christopher Reeve had won the role of Superman with his portrayal of the bumbling reporter Clark Kent—in horn-rimmed glasses, shoulders rounded into a slouch, and affecting what he called a "What's going on?" look.[7]

Reeve knew he would need to make the superhero character just as believable. Reeve was six feet four inches tall, but he was thin, weighing 188 pounds. The costumers wanted to make a Superman suit with Styrofoam muscles built in, but Reeve rejected the idea. "I had to get to a state where I would believe I was Superman," he said.[8] He hired bodybuilder David Prowse (who played Darth Vader in *Star Wars*) to help him achieve the look of a hero. After the first workout,

Reeve remembered feeling so ill that "I went into the locker room and heaved."[9]

He ate extra meals, drank special milkshakes, and ate lots of ice cream. He spent time each day lifting weights, designing his body into that of a believable superhero. He used a trampoline to practice realistic-looking takeoffs and landings. He started out tall and thin, but as the weeks went by, Reeve's shape gradually changed. His shoulders widened and his waist narrowed. After ten weeks of working out, Reeve had gained thirty-three pounds and added two inches to his chest. He was able to boast of real muscles.[10]

Superman was filmed mostly in England. During the time it took to make the movie, Reeve was under a contract that stated he would not act in any way that would discredit the Superman character. That part was easy. "I'm much more like Clark Kent," Reeve said.[11]

Other parts of the role were not as easy. During the filming, Reeve went through forty suits, changing whenever his costume became snagged or sweaty. It happened often, for Reeve insisted on doing his own stunt work. He spent much of his time in a rig that suspended him high in the air. When asked if the heights bothered him, Reeve shrugged off the danger, saying that after the first fifty feet it did not make any difference.[12]

In one scene, Superman was to fly holding his love interest Lois Lane, played by actress Margot Kidder, who also performed her own stunts. While in the rigging thirty feet above the floor, they suddenly heard the flying apparatus begin to crack. Reeve instinctively reached out his hand to catch the actress, as if he could safely fly them both away. "When I get in the costume something takes over," Reeve remembered with a laugh.[13]

Kidder's feelings about their relationship were affectionate. "He's like my brother," she said in a publicity interview. "He will be a major, major star someday," she predicted.[14]

Reeve did have trouble obeying some of the rules, however. His contract stated that he could not do any airplane flying while working on the film. The producers wanted to protect their investment by keeping their star safe from harm. Reeve ignored their worries. He would sneak away on his days off to a small

*Superman flies through the air, holding Lois Lane (played by Margot Kidder). Reeve and Kidder both performed their own stunts in the movie.*

club where he could fly over the English countryside without being seen by the movie crew or the press.[15]

With his growing career success, Reeve began having better luck finding interesting dates. Still, when out in public he tended to act more like Clark Kent than like a superhero. During a lunch break in October 1977, still dressed in his Superman costume, Reeve was choosing between soups, salads, and sandwiches in the cafeteria. As the line moved forward, he bumped into a pretty Englishwoman and stepped on her toes. The woman was Gae Exton, an executive with a modeling agency. "I made no first impression on her at all," Reeve said. "She just thought I was a large American person with black hair and red boots."[16] He was the one who was impressed.

Their courtship was not love at first sight. Exton had just separated from her husband, David Iveson, and was not ready for another relationship. After their first date, attending the play *The Belle of Amherst*, Exton was not sure where the relationship would lead. "I didn't want him to kiss me," she remembered. "I jumped out of the taxi, shouted 'Bye!' and ran away."[17] On the third date they did kiss.

Things were going well for Reeve, both professionally and personally. He was the star of a major film project, he was financially secure, and he was dating a beautiful woman. Would his good fortune last?

# A Star on the Subway

When *Superman* was released in December 1978, the producers held their breath and wondered: Would the audience like the film? Would the film make back its expensive, multimillion-dollar budget?

They did not have to wonder long. In its first week, *Superman* had already grossed $12 million in ticket sales. People flocked to theaters to see the movie about the baby from the planet Krypton who was sent to Earth and raised on a farm. Fans loved the dual personality of Clark Kent, who changes into Superman at the first sign of trouble.

Not only did audiences enjoy the movie, the critics agreed. A critic for *Newsweek* wrote, "Christopher Reeve's entire performance is a delight. Ridiculously good-looking, with a face as sharp and strong as an ax blade, his bumbling, fumbling Clark Kent and omnipotent Superman are simply two styles of gallantry and innocence."[1]

In one scene, Reeve clearly reveals the two different personalities of Clark Kent and Superman. Kent is about to identify himself to Lois Lane. He takes off his glasses, straightens his shoulders, and changes the look on his face to one of confidence—transforming himself into Superman as the audience watches.

The critic for the *New Yorker* wrote, "Christopher Reeve, the young actor chosen to play the lead in *Superman*, is the best reason to see the movie. He has an open-faced, deadpan style that's just right for a windup hero. . . . In this role, Reeve comes close to being a living equivalent of comic-strip art."[2]

Even Joe Shuster, one of the teenage creators of the original comic-book Superman, agreed. "I got chills. Chris Reeve has just the right touch of humor," he said. "He really *is* Superman."[3]

The blockbuster movie was nominated for three Academy Awards, winning the award for best visual effects. Reeve was suddenly a big star. Still, he was determined not to let success go to his head. "I did not want to be famous. I wanted to be at the top," Reeve said. "I thought they were separate."[4] He kept his old car, a Ford Pinto, and remained in his small apartment in Manhattan, refusing to make the move to Hollywood.

Reeve's success brought many offers for leading roles. To his agent's dismay, he turned down many parts after reading the scripts. He did not want to be part of projects he considered distasteful. One of

*Newsman Clark Kent always changes into Superman at the first sign of trouble.*

those was *American Gigolo*, which turned out to be great for actor Richard Gere's career.

Reeve felt he had earned the right to be choosy. "I've decided I'm not a bad actor after all," he said. "I'm reasonably happy, reasonably sane, reasonably positive. Enough people seem to like me, I like enough people—so I'll settle for that."[5]

His next movie choice was *Somewhere in Time*, with Jane Seymour (*Dr. Quinn, Medicine Woman*), though it was for much less money than other offers.[6] In this old-fashioned romance with a new twist, Reeve plays Richard Collier, a modern-day playwright who falls in love with a woman's photograph. The trouble is that the photograph was taken in the year 1912. He travels back in time, using mind control, to win her love.

While Reeve made this movie Gae Exton remained in London, though there were numerous phone calls back and forth. Filming took place on Mackinac Island, nestled between the upper and lower peninsulas of Michigan. This beautiful island is filled with the scent of tall pine trees. The island bans cars, so everyone walks or travels by bicycle or by horse and carriage. Many would consider this area a romantic, idyllic spot. But the numerous horses made Reeve uncomfortable because he was allergic to them. He spent his time on the island pedaling a bicycle to filming locations, after taking allergy pills!

Unfortunately, his discomfort was not rewarded. Critics panned the film. "Reeve looks too bulky, too big, too cartoonish for the role," wrote Gene Siskel.[7] It was the first sign that Reeve had been stereotyped as

*Grand Hotel on Mackinac Island. Reeve filmed the movie* Somewhere in Time *on this beautiful island in Michigan. No cars are allowed on the island, so many people travel by horse and carriage. Because of his allergy to horses, Reeve preferred to use a bicycle.*

a superhero. "The qualities that made him such an ideal Superman—look absurd here," said another.[8]

Reeve had the opportunity to play his "ideal" role again. His earlier contract committed him to a *Superman* sequel, which was already under way. He also took on a new role in his personal life: On December 20, 1979, during time off from filming *Superman II*, Reeve and Gae Exton had a son, Matthew, in London's Welbeck Hospital.

Of course, Reeve needed time to adjust to the part of "father." Reeve became a good parent, though some of the press were amused to ask the public: "Imagine, *Superman* changing *diapers*!"[9]

Reeve was still Superman to his fans. He often made publicity appearances and enjoyed talking to young fans. He left his Superman costume at home and spoke about Superman's inner character, rather than about his super powers. "They should be looking for Superman's qualities—courage, determination, modesty, humor—in themselves," Reeve said, stating the ideals he used to guide his own life.[10]

When Matthew was old enough to crawl and pull himself up onto furniture, Reeve and Exton decided they needed a bigger home. They moved into a penthouse apartment with a rooftop garden on New York's Upper West Side. Sailing pictures and Broadway play posters decorated the walls, but there was no image of Superman displayed. They also rented a townhouse in London.

When in New York, Reeve spent much of his time at home with his young son.[11] He enjoyed appearing in shows Matthew could see on television. As a guest on *The Muppet Show*, he made fun of his Superman character. He also played Prince Charming with actress Bernadette Peters as Cinderella on Shelley Duvall's *Faerie Tale Theatre*. Not all appearances were for his son's enjoyment, though. He and Robin Williams were able to work together in an appearance on *Saturday Night Live*.

Reeve was now a celebrity. Once, while waiting for the subway, a woman approached Reeve. "What is the point of becoming a movie star if you're going to take the subway?" she asked, then walked away. Telling the story later, Reeve exclaimed, "I haven't taken the subway since!"[12]

Reeve completed the filming of *Superman II*, again performing many dangerous stunts. This time his salary was doubled to $500,000. Once again he was required to hang in the contraption of metal and wires for flying scenes. On one occasion he dangled over rapids just above Niagara Falls. Other shooting locales were Norway, France, and even the island of St. Lucia in the West Indies for one romantic scene with Superman and Lois Lane in the rain forest.

After the successful opening in June 1981, Reeve was asked about his future plans. He admitted he might agree to another *Superman* sequel. "I owe Superman," he explained. "If it hadn't been for him . . . I'd probably be out there parking cars."[13]

While always acknowledging that first major role as his stepping-stone to success, Reeve found it was also a role that would forever haunt him.

# Escape from the Cape

After completing *Superman II*, Reeve decided to take a break from films. He acted in three plays at the Williamstown Theatre Festival in Massachusetts during the summer of 1980. He earned only $225 a week. He enjoyed being in a small town, wandering down the main street in his bare feet with no one bothering him. He also liked playing the classic parts live onstage, using his summer breaks as a regular retreat from film work. He returned to Williamstown almost every summer until 1994.

Reeve continued to enjoy challenging sports as well, such as skiing, sailing, and flying. In fact, flying began taking up more and more of his time. He owned a glider and a twin-engine Beechcraft. He used his own plane instead of the commercial airlines both for transportation to publicity appearances and, he later described, "as an escape hatch."[1]

Once he flew four friends to Nantucket. They took the short jaunt to escape busy New York City and enjoy a leisurely day visiting the whaling museum. He was happy his friends and family were confident in his piloting ability. "I used to think that if the passengers weren't just hanging out the window and thrilled with the whole thing that there was something wrong," he said. "But now I take it as a compliment when somebody just sits back and goes to sleep. It means they trust you."[2] Reeve proclaimed his love of flying in many interviews. He felt that if his acting career were suddenly to end, he could see himself working as a pilot at a commercial airline.[3]

With another Superman film under his belt, Reeve once again tried to avoid being typecast as a superhero. He deliberately picked roles that had a very different image from Superman. He turned down many lucrative offers, choosing instead to act in the Broadway play *The Fifth of July*, which opened in 1980. "I can't just say 'I'm not Superman, I'm an actor,'" he explained. "I have to prove it."[4]

Reeve played a depressed Vietnam War veteran, withdrawn from the world around him. The character is also a homosexual and a paraplegic who lost both legs in the war. Reeve researched the role by visiting a hospital for paraplegics and observing how they walk with artificial legs. The paraplegic aspect of the role was not the only thing that made it hard for audiences who identified Reeve with Superman. They were surprised by the very first scene—Reeve is sitting onstage in a wheelchair and his boyfriend gives him a big kiss on the lips.

Critics gave poor reviews of opening night. They liked Christopher Reeve as Superman onscreen, but they felt he was more like Clark Kent onstage. This comparison with Reeve's Superman role would continue throughout his life.

Even without the critics' support, Reeve stuck with the role, and he felt he improved with every performance. He found time to relax by taking short ski trips to Vermont or by playing cards with his neighbor, the singer Carly Simon. He enjoyed taking Matthew to Central Park and spending quiet evenings at home with Exton. He continued playing the piano, practicing as much as an hour a day. In fact, in a 1981 appearance on *The Merv Griffin Show*, Reeve played a piano composition he had written, *Ode to the Sailplane*.

Reeve left the cast of *Fifth of July* in June 1981 to return to the Williamstown Theatre Festival for the role of Achilles in *The Greeks*. By this time, *Superman II* had opened in the theaters, and it became another box office hit. Many people felt it was unique among films in that the sequel was even better than the original movie. Reeve and Exton were often separated because of his film schedules, but they were together for the opening gala.

The critics were friendly. "In his two roles, Reeve is even better than he was in the first film, boyish and mannish, torn between his love for Lois and his love and duty to mankind," wrote one reviewer.[5]

While appreciative of the clout the Superman role

gave him, Reeve was determined not to be typecast as a superhero. Of numerous offered parts, the one he chose to play next was a psychopathic character in the movie *Deathtrap*, a murder mystery with Michael Caine and Dyan Cannon. The reviews were not bad, but the public did not rush out to see the movie, and it did not do well at theaters. Reeve did not seem to mind. He had never expected stardom and would have enjoyed acting in regional theaters.

Reeve then took another unlikable role, playing a corrupt priest in *Monsignor*. First, he researched the part by attending a Catholic retreat in New Jersey. Then he was off to Rome, Italy, for filming. Instead of riding as a first-class passenger on a commercial airline, Reeve decided to fly himself across the Atlantic. It was a dangerous feat. As Reeve flew across the ocean, he eyed his gas gauge closely. At one point, he listened as a ground station in Greenland radioed flight information. If the data were correct, he would run out of gas and crash into the cold sea before reaching his destination. For the next thirty long minutes, Reeve's heart beat quickly as he checked and recalculated the figures. Fortunately, the first figures were wrong and Reeve landed safely.

In *Monsignor*, Reeve plays a young chaplain who falls in love with a nun. His character falls prey to greed, using Mafia money for contributions to the Vatican. The reviews were terrible. "Only his best friend or his best accountant can explain why the talented Reeve signed on for this ecclesiastical geek of a movie," wrote one reviewer.[6] Reeve was not the only one to take the fall for the movie. The entire production was ridiculed by the entertainment press.

Reeve's filming schedule often put his family on a different continent. Exton spent most of her time with Matthew at their home in London. Still, when Reeve was in New York City, he did not have to spend a lot of time at home alone. His doorbell was often ringing. During the day, third graders from a nearby school might come by to ask if Superman could come out to play. At night, it would be Robin Williams at the door, ready to take Reeve out to party in the city. The two friends were as close as ever and often joked about both being aliens visiting planet Earth. Reeve was the fellow from planet Krypton, and Williams was starring as the alien Mork from Ork in the hit television comedy *Mork and Mindy*.

*Superman I* and *II* had been big hits, but *Superman III* was to be a different story. Reeve had come a long way since his days as an unknown actor. Now that he was Superman the star, he received $2 million and top billing. Even so, he was not the highest paid actor in the movie. Comedian Richard Pryor was given $4 million for his role as villain Lex Luthor's dim-witted sidekick.

When the film was released in June 1983, *Superman* fans flocked to see the newest sequel. The film made $13 million in its first week. However, this movie was more of a comedy showcasing Pryor's stand-up act, rather than a drama like the first two *Superman* movies. Word-of-mouth reports were that it did not live up to the earlier movies. It lasted only about a month at theaters.

*Superman III, which opened in movie theaters in 1983, was more of a comedy showcasing comedian Richard Pryor (left) than a superhero action film.*

Reeve had gone through with his commitment to the film. He remained true to his word, even though he, too, felt the movie was not up to the standards set by the previous *Superman* movies. He vowed never to return to his Superman character. "I've flown, become evil, loved, stopped and turned the world backward. I've faced my peers, I've befriended children and small animals, and I've rescued cats from trees," he said. "What is there left for Superman to do that hasn't already been done?"[7]

Soon after the release of *Superman III* came the announcement that Reeve and Exton were to have another child. During the filming in Yugoslavia of *The Aviator*, Reeve received word that Exton was on her way to the hospital. He rushed back to London in time for the birth of their daughter, Alexandra.

Once again Reeve was faced with a choice of film roles. To his agent's surprise, Reeve turned down a million-dollar offer for *The Bounty*. Instead he accepted a little more than $100,000 to play Basil Ransom, a Mississippi lawyer in *The Bostonians*, starring Vanessa Redgrave. Reeve considered himself a serious actor. He did not want to be caught up in the current trend of films presenting tough, macho actors in roles carried more by the action and violence than by the story's plot. "I wanted to be an actor, not run around with a machine gun," he explained.[8]

Though his agent did not agree, this time Reeve had made the right career decision. To prepare for the role, he read the original novel written by Henry James in 1886. He recorded speeches of a Mississippi lawyer and politician, Haley Barbour, and practiced his southern accent.

The movie was shot on Martha's Vineyard, where Reeve's brother Ben had a home and where Reeve had sailed as a child with his father. There were many early mornings when Reeve would get up at dawn to sail near Cape Cod before work began. He enjoyed the quiet time alone, breathing in the salty sea air. Still, the daring side of him yearned for adventure. One day he went parasailing, gliding high in the air while being pulled behind a motorboat. Suddenly, his parachute broke loose. Reeve fell from the sky, plummeting into the shallow water below. It was a terrible fall that

*Christopher Reeve with Gae Exton and their two children, Matthew and Alexandra, return to London after a skiing vacation in 1985.*

could easily have left him dead or with serious injuries. Reeve came out of the accident with only bruised ribs. Still, the near tragedy did not hamper his risk-taking. "That's living to me," Reeve explained. "If nature decides to bat you around on the sea or in the air, you know what you have to do to survive it. It's not like show business, where people can be devious and manipulative."[9]

In *The Bostonians*, Reeve sported long hair and a mustache, in no way resembling Superman. Critics managed to continue weaving in that role comparison, favorably this time. "Mr. Reeve makes you forget his Superman achievements 'faster than a speeding bullet,'" wrote one reviewer.[10]

Reeve enjoyed acting with Redgrave so much that when she asked him to appear with her in London in a play based on another Henry James novel, *The Aspern Papers*, he agreed. It also offered Reeve the opportunity to spend time with his family in London.

Reeve returned to the Williamstown Theatre Festival for the summer and was able to enjoy the new home he had purchased in a quiet, wooded area outside town. The rustic home sits on more than thirty-five acres of land, and there was plenty of room to park his glider. Reeve began buying thoroughbred horses and taking riding lessons during the day. He took medication for his allergies. Reeve also splurged on a forty-six-foot yacht, custom-built with seven-foot bunks that comfortably fit his height. He named this boat *The Sea Angel* and immediately sailed it four hundred miles from Long Island, New York, to Maine.

Reeve enjoyed an active lifestyle. Rather than lying

on the beach sunbathing, he preferred sports that involved endurance and skill. He spent many days challenging himself with tennis, windsurfing, flying, sailing, and horseback riding.

Immediately after the summer season, Reeve flew to Hungary to film the television movie *Anna Karenina* with Jacqueline Bisset. Compared with what he was used to, Hungary seemed primitive. There were few bathrooms in the area where they were filming, the weather was cold and damp, and the crew lived on salted meat.

Anna, the main character in the movie, leaves a loveless marriage to live with her true love. She is still cheated of happiness because her husband refuses to let her see her only son, telling the child that his mother is dead. Reeve remembered reading the book for a class at Cornell. The story was so compelling that he could not to put the book down, and he had finished it in one weekend.

When it aired in 1985, the historical drama was up against two popular television shows, *Who's the Boss?* and *The A-Team*. Despite its high critical appeal and widespread promotion, *Anna Karenina* did not draw a large audience.

Reeve began feeling the effects of being selective with roles. Often, the parts he chose did not offer a lot of money, but now he had three homes, a yacht, a number of planes, and a family to support. To be able to keep all those possessions and still provide his family with the lifestyle they were now accustomed to, Reeve decided to don the cape once again.

# "Make a Difference"

Reeve may have wanted the money it would bring, but he set certain conditions before agreeing to *Superman IV*. After the lukewarm response to *Superman III*, he wanted to personally approve the script as well as help direct the film. Reeve would receive $4 million for his work in both *Superman IV* and another film of his choice.[1]

*Street Smart* was the movie Reeve chose to do first. "It was time for a contemporary role," Reeve said of his decision, "a real person today."[2] In this film, he plays a journalist who writes a fictional story about life in the inner city but publishes it as fact in a magazine. This quickly gets him into trouble when people think he is protecting a man accused of murder. No one believes that he made up the story. This film was not to be another shallow example of how good conquers evil. "It is about personal ethics versus the pressure to succeed," Reeve described. "I felt it would be interesting to play a man who is really quite lost, very weak, dishonest, and stupid in many ways."[3]

To prepare for the role of urban writer, Reeve rode along in a patrol car with police in New York City. "We always had an escape plan and the cops protected me," Reeve explained. "I was near the action on busts and raids."[4] Reeve's costar, Morgan Freeman, earned an Academy Award nomination for his role, but the movie was not successful at the theaters.

In between filming *Street Smart* and *Superman IV*, Reeve made his first political appearance, campaigning for a Vermont senator, Democrat Patrick Leahy. Ever since the first *Superman* movie became a success, Reeve had appeared in his Superman cape for causes he supported, such as the Make-A-Wish Foundation, which asked him to visit terminally ill children. He had learned that the Superman image could be used productively to benefit others, and he believed that he had a responsibility to use his fame to help society.[5] Since Reeve agreed with many of Senator Leahy's positions, he agreed to speak in Burlington, encouraging voters to choose the man who wanted to pass laws for a clean environment and arms control. Leahy was reelected.

Reeve's interest in protecting the environment and world peace did not stop there. He made sure this theme was woven into the new *Superman* script. In this movie, Superman's quest is to round up all the nuclear weapons and destroy them by hurling them into the sun. The movie's title would reflect this theme as well. Rather than being released merely as the fourth sequel, the title was *Superman IV: The Quest for Peace*.

Reeve arranged for his children to have small parts in the movie. Matthew and Alexandra played children trapped in the path of a twisting tornado. The children were on the set quite often, even on days when they were not involved in the filming. They enjoyed spending time with their dad, laughing and squealing in delight when he would pick them up and swing them around or search for them in a quick game of hide-and-seek.

Reeve liked being with his children and loved his role as their father, but his ten-year relationship with Gae Exton, their mother, was over. The children lived in London with Exton during the school year and in Williamstown with Reeve in the summer. Knowing how this situation echoed his own childhood, Reeve hoped that he and Exton would be able to remain on good terms and work out arrangements that would be the best for the children. "For now, they understand that they have two homes and that they'll be fully loved and accepted in each," he told an interviewer.[6]

The press often speculated on reasons for the breakup, but Reeve insisted the reports were false. "It was just a growing awareness that we were the wrong people for each other," he said.[7]

Five months later, Reeve met the woman who was the right match. On June 30, 1987, Reeve went with friends to a nightclub in Williamstown. He sat at a table in the front and became enraptured with the beautiful woman with large brown eyes who was singing "The Music That Makes Me Dance."[8] After her number, Reeve went up and introduced himself.

It was not love at first sight—for her. Dana Morosini, an actress from Scarsdale, New York, turned Reeve down a number of times. He persisted, and it finally paid off. "We ended up talking for an hour," Reeve described their first evening together. "We didn't get a drink, we didn't sit down, we didn't move. Everything just vanished around us."[9]

"I didn't expect to really fall in love," said Morosini about the romance.[10] Over the summer she got to know the Hollywood superstar as he truly was. "I realized he wasn't just this movie star," she said. "I found that he was very much like me."[11]

They did have very similar backgrounds. Morosini had acted and sung in many high school plays, then traveled to Valencia, California, to earn her master's degree from California's Institute of the Arts. From there, she went on to play small parts in off-Broadway productions, as well as acting in television commercials. The summer of 1987 was her first at the Williamstown Theatre Festival, and it did not take long for her to be noticed by Reeve, who was quickly smitten. "It was a case of what happens to you when you're not looking," Reeve explained. "Happiness sneaks up."[12]

Reeve's personal life was going well, but his career was faltering. *Superman IV* was not the huge success it was expected to be. This was blamed on the fact that the producers had run out of money and released

*When Christopher Reeve met actress/singer Dana Morosini, he was immediately smitten.*

the film before it was finished. Close scrutiny reveals that when Superman is flying through the air, the same flying sequence is used four times. There are even spots where wires are faintly visible.

Still, the public clung to Reeve's image as the true heroic character. On one occasion, Reeve and a friend parked their bicycles outside a local tavern in New York City and went inside. When they came out and discovered that their bikes had been stolen, the two split up to search the area. Reeve ran three blocks, catching up with one of the thieves. Reeve grabbed him off the bike and threw him onto the sidewalk.

"He looked up," Reeve said as he later described the real-life action scene, "and [he] screamed, 'Oh, no, Superman! I'm sorry!'"[13]

That thief was not the only one who felt Reeve had the powers of Superman. On November 22, 1987, Reeve received a call from Chilean playwright Ariel Dorfman, who pleaded for Reeve's help. Dorfman was a political activist supported by Amnesty International, an organization dedicated to helping political prisoners. His plan was for Reeve to fly to Chile, then ruled by General Augusto Pinochet, a dictator who ignored the country's constitution, imposed strict censorship, and sponsored death squads. Pinochet's regime threatened actors and directors with execution if they did not leave the country. Dorfman's dangerous plan was to have Reeve lead a rally to help save those actors. "I can't guarantee your life," Dorfman said. "They might want to kill Superman to make a point."[14]

Reeve accepted the risky mission. "How do you answer when someone says, 'We really think you could directly save the lives of seventy-seven people'?" Reeve explained. "I couldn't think of anything more important than that."[15] He arrived in Santiago on November 30, 1987. Local papers proclaimed his arrival with a picture of Superman carrying Pinochet in his arms and flying the dictator out of the country.[16] Young actors walked the streets of the city wearing T-shirts with a bull's-eye target and the words "Shoot Me First." Tension mounted when the Chilean Actors' Union received a threatening message. Reeve walked into the hot stadium for the rally, unsure of what would happen next. Sweat dripped down his back. The stands were filled with people, yelling and chanting. Suddenly, police arrived, spraying tear gas into the crowd and forcing them to disperse.

The organizers refused to give up. They quickly arranged for a new rally location nearby. Reeve walked into the building, this time surrounded by six body guards. The large garage was packed with thousands of people. Some grabbed at him, tearing off pieces of his clothing when they recognized him as the actor who played Superman. Reeve thought back to the anti-war rallies at Cornell. "[In college] there is the basic assumption that nothing is really going to happen to you," Reeve said. "But this was real life."[17]

After fighting his way to the stage, Reeve spoke to the crowd, reading from a letter that had been signed by many actors and actresses back in the United States. The crowd cheered and sang "He Will Fall," a revolutionary song. The next day, the death squad order was canceled.

"Reeve deserves the primary credit for saving eighty-eight lives," said David Hinkley, a former representative of Amnesty International.[18] "This was not Superman to the rescue," Reeve insisted. "It was me as a private citizen, and as an actor in a country where we take the freedom to perform for granted, helping fellow professionals in a country where they do not."[19]

In 1989, Reeve, along with Susan Sarandon, Alec Baldwin, and other celebrities, cofounded the Creative Coalition, a group concerned with the environment, homelessness, and the arts. Once Reeve

In 1987, "Superman" showed his courage and his power beyond the movie screen: Christopher Reeve flew to Chile, where the country's dictator had threatened all actors with death. Reeve joined other international stars to speak on behalf of the Chilean actors, and the death threat was canceled.

realized his capabilities as an activist, he also became independently involved in social issues. In between acting projects, such as the film *Switching Channels* and the television movie *The Great Escape II: The Untold Story*, he kept busy with other projects he believed in. He was among thousands of animal rights activists who rallied in Washington, D.C., on June 10, 1990, to promote the humane treatment of animals, including those in research labs.

Reeve returned to Williamstown to protest the proposed building of a coal-burning power plant. Some criticized his involvement. One reporter wrote, "Anyone who's a hero on the silver screen can expound on just about anything and the star-struck public will lap it up. . . . There's something frightening about all this."[20]

Reeve disagreed, saying, "If you can make a difference, you should do it."[21] He continued making sure his voice was heard. He recorded a series of public service announcements, as well as narrated a documentary for the Discovery Channel, *Black Tide*, about the deadly oil spill from the tanker *Exxon Valdez*. He went to Washington, D.C., to press for passage of the Clean Air Act. He was most involved in issues he felt were important to the world, such as toxic waste, recycling, clean water, deforestation, and global warming.

When Reeve attended the twentieth reunion of his Princeton Country Day School class in 1990, he was given the Alumni Award for "extensive involvement in human services." The headmaster, Duncan Alling, presented Reeve with a plaque. "Volunteer work is a

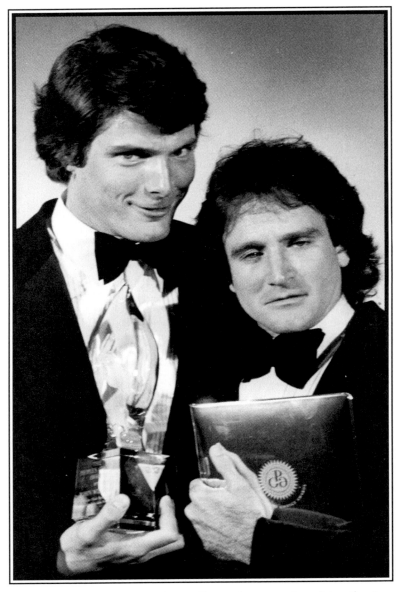

*Christopher Reeve and Robin Williams became close friends when they were roommates in college. Here, Reeve presents Williams with the 1979 People's Choice Award for Favorite Male Performer.*

very important value to promote," he said. "[Reeve] has demonstrated extraordinary effort in this area."[22]

Just as Reeve's passion for environmental and political causes grew, so did his relationship with Dana Morosini. They spent as much time together as possible. They would go sailing together and go on long horseback rides. They went out dancing and were often seen laughing together. One evening in December 1991, over a candlelit dinner, Reeve and Morosini said at the same time, "Let's get married!"[23]

On April 11, 1992, with Matthew and Alexandra, now twelve and eight years old, as best man and maid of honor, Christopher Reeve and Dana Morosini were married. They were not able to take a honeymoon, since Dana was in a play in New York City.

After their baby son, Will, was born, the Reeves bought a nineteenth-century farmhouse in New York's Westchester County, an hour from New York City. Still, they could not bear to sell the house in Williamstown.

While he was busy on the home front, Reeve's acting career had slowed. He compared his own career to that of his friend Robin Williams. "He was Popeye at the same time I was Superman," he said with a laugh. "[Now] Robin is jet-propelled, and I am paddling alongside in a canoe."[24]

7

# "Superman Is Down"

In 1992, Reeve campaigned for Democrats Bill Clinton and Al Gore for president and vice president. Meeting at the New Jersey shore, Reeve and Gore picked up litter scattered along the beaches while promoting Gore's vow to clean up the environment.

Reeve continued making movies for television, such as *The Rose and the Jackal*, *Mortal Sins*, and *The Sea Wolf*. He appeared on television shows, including *The Reporters* and *The World's Greatest Stunts*. He acted onstage in Shakespeare's *The Winter's Tale* at New York's Public Theatre and went on a national tour with Julie Hagerty in a two-character play, *Love Letters*.

Though Reeve agreed that he had been perfect for

*Activist Christopher Reeve works hard for the causes he believes in. In 1992 he showed his support for a clean environment and for vice presidential candidate Al Gore. Reeve and Gore joined members of Clean Ocean Action at the annual beach cleanup in Sandy Hook, New Jersey.*

the part of Superman at age twenty-four, he laughed when he thought of how many sit-ups it would take to get into that same shape. "People don't want to see Superman with a spare tire hanging over his yellow belt," he said.[1]

Reeve waited for a role that would return him to the big screen. Finally, the call came. English producer James Ivory sent Reeve a script for *The Remains of the Day*. He wanted Reeve to play Lewis, the American character who, just before World War II, tries to convince an English nobleman that Nazi Germany is not interested in peace.

It was a small but important role in the movie about two house servants—played by Anthony Hopkins and Emma Thompson—who hide their love for each other. The film was a huge critical success, drawing large audiences for what was considered an "art film." The film received eight Oscar nominations. "I don't regard that as my movie—I was a visitor—but it's the best movie I've ever been in," Reeve said in 1994.[2]

Offers again arrived at his door. Reeve signed film contracts for *Speechless* with Michael Keaton and Geena Davis, for *Village of the Damned* with Kirstie Alley, and for *Above Suspicion*, in which his wife, Dana, had a small role as well.

Before beginning the busy filming schedule, Reeve visited Cornell for the first time since he left the campus in 1974. He offered acting tips to drama students, giving advice on auditions. "You've got to walk into the room like you're claiming the part," Reeve said.[3] His lecture also discussed the importance of being responsible members of society, using his volunteer activities as examples.

The self-confidence Reeve projected was not an act. He had come to believe in his own capabilities—not only in his acting but in all other pursuits as well. Once, when flying a plane in England, Reeve found himself in bad weather conditions. He kept his wits while making a crash landing in a country field. With the plane on the ground, Reeve took a deep breath and opened the pilot's door. He walked through the field to a nearby cottage and knocked on the door, asking to make a phone call. "Why do you look so familiar?" the woman asked him. "I'm Superman," he answered.[4]

In addition to flying, Reeve was becoming more and more interested in horseback riding, often practicing for several hours a day (after taking medicine to counteract his allergies, which eventually disappeared). He began jumping, which requires excellent timing and balance between horse and rider. He learned to hold the reins just right: loose enough to give the horse the room it needed to jump, but tight enough to keep command of the animal. He learned to apply pressure with his legs, moving together with the horse in a balanced rhythm.

Reeve took his riding seriously and began entering competitions in this sport. He won a novice event in Vermont and placed third at the New England novice championships. As was his habit, Reeve found another important cause to support—equestrian safety. A picture of Reeve riding his horse, Denver, was made into a poster with this caption: "In films I play an invincible hero. But in real life I wouldn't think of riding without a helmet."[5] The poster was never distributed.

*Speechless* was released in December 1994. In a promotional interview, both Reeve and Keaton—who had starred in two of the *Batman* movies—promised they would never again wear the capes of their superhero characters.

*Village of the Damned* opened only a few months later, and Reeve was already busy researching his part as a detective in *Above Suspicion*. Because his character would be injured in a shootout and then become wheelchair bound, Reeve visited a spinal cord trauma unit to see how people with such injuries underwent

*As Reeve's love of horseback riding grew, he often practiced for several hours a day and began to enter competitions in the sport.*

rehabilitation and learned to use a wheelchair. He felt uncomfortable after speaking to the doctors and patients about spinal injuries. "You see how easily it can happen," he said. "You think, 'God, it could happen to anybody.'"[6] In one scene in the film, Reeve's character turns to his younger brother and says, "I'm paralyzed." This statement was to become prophetic.

Reeve was vibrant and active and happily married to Dana. "She is my life force," Reeve said.[7] He spent as much time as possible playing with young Will. "[We enjoy] sailing on our boat . . . and throwing rocks in the water down at the dock . . . , tramping out in the woods . . . looking for owls," Reeve said.[8] That would soon change.

In early spring 1995, Reeve gave his wife a butterfly

house and a batch of wildflower seeds for her birthday. Dana planted the seeds but doubted the hard ground would ever give way to wildflower sprouts. The garden was still bare in late May when the Reeve family left home to attend a riding event in Virginia. It would be Reeve's last riding competition.

Reeve flew Dana and Will to Virginia for the Memorial Day weekend event. On that Friday afternoon, Reeve practiced riding on his new horse, Eastern Express, whom he affectionately called "Buck." Reeve walked the course for the next day's cross-country jumping event. There would be a series of jumps and hazards to cross, and he would be timed for speed and judged on technique. Reeve walked from jump to jump, looking for possible problems, such as uneven ground, unusual spacing between jumps, or even shadows that may trick the eye. Over and over, he checked the course, committing it to memory.

The next morning, May 27, 1995, Reeve woke to a beautiful spring day in the country. The skies were blue, dotted with puffy clouds. He dressed in his navy jacket, riding pants, and tall boots, with a velvet-covered helmet and a padded vest added for safety. He left his wife with their toddler and traveled to Commonwealth Park, where rolling acres of green fields and sparse woods are outlined with white fencing. The Blue Ridge Mountains loomed in the distance. Once again, Reeve checked the course. After adjusting his outfit and rechecking the horse's gear, he led the horse out of his stall and mounted, heading to a warm-up area.

The two-mile course was set up with fifteen jumps

of stone walls or wooden-rail fencing. When it was his turn, Reeve readied himself, gave Eastern Express a command, and the two set off. After the first two jumps were cleared easily, the pair headed for the third jump, a set of wooden timbers in a zigzag pattern a little more than three feet high—normally a simple jump. "The horse was coming into the fence beautifully," described Lisa Reid, a horse trainer who was a spectator at the event. "The rhythm was fine and Chris was fine, and they were going at a good pace."[9]

In a jumping competition, the combination of horse and rider is very important. Any flaw in either of their performances could result in disaster. No one knows what caused Eastern Express to stop, but he did. "The horse put his front feet over the fence, but his hind feet never left the ground," Reid said. "Chris is such a big man. He was going forward, his head over the top of the horse's head. . . . But the horse . . . backed off the jump."[10]

Reeve could not stop his own momentum. He was propelled forward, bringing the bridle, the bit, and the reins with him. He hit his head on the fence and then on the ground below. A judge quickly alerted the medics, saying, "Superman is down."[11]

Because his hands had become tangled in the bridle, Reeve was not able to put out an arm to break his fall. Instead of suffering a possible sprained wrist, Reeve landed straight on his head.

Christopher Reeve, forty-two years old, was paralyzed from the neck down.

# A Sign of Hope

Christopher Reeve's six-foot-four body suddenly seemed small and fragile. His face was pale and his limbs were limp.

After being resuscitated by an anesthesiologist who happened to be among the spectators, Reeve was taken by ambulance to the local hospital in Culpeper, Virginia. From there, he was put into a helicopter, ironically named *Pegasus* after the winged horse in Greek mythology. He was immediately flown to the University of Virginia Medical Center and placed under the care of a skilled neurosurgeon, Dr. John Jane. Dana and Will soon arrived at the hospital, as did both of Reeve's parents and his brother Benjamin. Gae Exton flew from England, bringing their two children, Matthew and Alexandra.

*After his riding accident in May 1995, Reeve was flown by helicopter to the University of Virginia Medical Center.*

Just as the family had quickly gathered, so did members of the press. They were held off for a few days with the information that Reeve was being closely watched. Finally it was announced that he had fractured the first and second vertebrae at the base of his skull. Doctors admitted he was fighting for his life. He was unconscious and could not breathe on his own, dependent on a machine called a ventilator for every breath.

When Reeve's mother learned the extent of her son's condition, she felt that they should "pull the plug," meaning unhook the ventilator that was keeping him alive. "She knew what an active life I'd always led—that for me being active and being alive were the same thing," Reeve explained. "In the past I would have agreed with her."[1]

The rest of the family wanted to wait, to leave the decision to Reeve himself. He regained consciousness four days later, confused and unable to remember what had happened. He thought, "This can't be my life. There's been a mistake."[2] When Dana came into his room, Reeve mouthed to her, "Maybe we should let me go." Dana was crying, but she looked him in the eye and said, "You're still you, and I love you."[3] Those words may have saved his life.

Dana spent as much time as possible with her husband, sleeping in his room so she would be there if he woke up during the night. Reeve also had some support from his good friend Robin Williams. "I was hanging upside down [in a hospital bed] . . . and I saw a blue scrub hat and yellow gown and heard this Russian accent," Reeve remembered.[4]

"I said, 'I'm going to haff to, just go down, hold on, I'm just goink to . . . ,'" described Williams. "Then [Reeve] realized who it was, and his eyes lit up, and he started to laugh."[5]

"[He was] being some insane Russian doctor," Reeve said. "I laughed, and I knew I was going to be all right."[6]

There was a tremendous outpouring of sympathy from the public, who wished him well. Dana had kept silent for days, but she knew she must address the press and give her husband's fans some information. "Much of his day is spent listening to messages from well-wishers. I can't begin to express how important these are to him," she said at a press conference. She singled out the messages sent from others with spinal cord injuries. "Chris is particularly heartened by the brave and thoughtful letters sent by the many people who have suffered similar injuries."[7]

"You are a Superman and you will pull through this like the hero that you are," read one on-line message. "Almost three years ago . . . a spinal cord injury not too different from yours left me hospitalized. . . . It was the darkest moment of my life. I've come miles since that moment, and life is every bit as enjoyable and worthwhile as it ever was," said another.[8]

Dana summed up the family's situation. "He is a fighter and a survivor of the first order, but this has to be the toughest challenge he has ever faced. I know it is mine."[9]

Later, Reeve would describe what happened to his neck—"the hangman's injury"—"It was as if I'd been hanged, cut down and sent to rehab."[10] On June 5, 1995, Dr. Jane performed surgery to fuse the vertebrae of Reeve's spine back together, using rings and wires and bone fragments from Reeve's hip to reconnect his head to his body. The operation was to keep the bones in line so they could not do more damage to the spinal cord. After the surgery, Reeve thanked the doctor for giving him life.[11]

One month later, Reeve was able to sit upright when strapped into a chair, his neck supported by a brace. He could breathe for a few minutes without his ventilator. When it was removed, his first speech was "Testing—one, two, three."[12] Dana remained at his

*Dr. John A. Jane, chairman of the Department of Neurosurgery at the University of Virginia, performed a delicate operation to fuse Reeve's spinal cord back together.*

side, watching television with him or reading him his many letters.

On June 28, 1995, Reeve left the University of Virginia Medical Center to begin rehabilitation at the Kessler Institute in New Jersey. He could feel some sensation when touched, though he was not able to move any of his limbs on his own. He could now speak a little, through the use of a portable ventilator.

Reeve's mother, Barbara Johnson, met with the press, issuing thanks to all who helped her son after the accident. "The list begins with the anesthesiologist . . . who happened to be standing by the jump in Culpeper," she said. "His skillful administration of CPR literally saved Chris's life."[13] She went on to include the emergency medical staff and the doctors at the University of Virginia Medical Center. "One of the sweet things was how Dr. Mo, as we called him [Dr. Mohan Nadkarni], took little Will, three-year-old Will, under his wing and cared for him for a while so Dana could be with Chris."[14]

Of course, the family was also worried about little Will, whose father lay motionless in a hospital bed. "He had this fear, as small children do, that he would catch his father's illness or that I would get sick," Dana said.[15]

Often, young children find it difficult to express their fears. Will found a way through role-playing. He rode happily on his hobbyhorse but then suddenly fell off, saying, "'I hurt my neck,' and I would say, 'Well, your neck is okay, but Dad's neck is not,'" Dana said. "Eventually, on a very courageous day, he said, 'I want to see Daddy.'"[16]

By July, Reeve was still using the ventilator, but he was speaking much more clearly and was able to use an electric-powered wheelchair. It was time for his family to return to their daily lives while Reeve continued his rehabilitation at Kessler.

Barbara Johnson had been spending much of her time answering the thousands of letters and gifts her son had received from concerned people around the world. How could she now return to normal life? Back home in Princeton, Reeve's mother found a sense of peace rowing across Lake Carnegie. "There was release and forgetfulness in that six-mile trip to the end of the lake and back three or four times a week," she said. "It was a godsend."[17]

Dana Reeve also struggled with emotions as she returned home without her husband. As she drove up to their farmhouse, six weeks after the day the Reeves had set out for Virginia, she was amazed at the sight before her. The wildflower seeds her husband had given her were now a blaze of color surrounding the butterfly house. "The flowers were out of control," Dana said. "They were literally wildflowers gone wild. It was a real sign of hope."[18]

# "Nothing Is Impossible"

$T$he next few months would determine the type of life Christopher Reeve would lead. Could he rise to the challenge, or would he feel overwhelmed and give up?

At first, Reeve was even embarrassed, as if the accident had been a personal failure. "For some reason I didn't get my hands down and break my fall. I'm an idiot," he said later.[1] He felt as though he ruined not only his own life but his entire family's as well.

Reeve was also afraid of rehabilitation. Being so dependent on his ventilator and on the care of others made him feel helpless.[2] He was frightened of small things that used to be normal daily activities, such as taking a shower. He worried that water might get into the ventilator. Even the wheelchair terrified him. When he was moved from his bed to his chair, he was afraid he might be dropped. His arms and legs were strapped down and a seat belt put on. The change to an upright position might cause a sudden spike in blood pressure. The entire process would give him a panic attack.[3]

Eventually, Reeve's characteristic determination took over. He drew on his athletic background and began pushing himself to the limit. "I had to be as disciplined about my body as I had been about learning to fly a plane, or sail a boat, or ride a horse," Reeve said.[4]

The doctors told him the numbers they used to measure his progress. They found this motivated their patient, bringing out his competitiveness. One test monitored the force he used to breathe in. At first, Reeve could not even move the dial, but he would try over and over until he finally made it budge. Days later he could breathe on his own for a few minutes, and he worked to increase that time. "Sports were an important part of my life, and I actually regard this as a different kind of sport," he said.[5]

The first thing he wanted to do was get off the ventilator. Reeve later described what he referred to as the "breathe or die" method of rehabilitation.[6] The medical staff would unplug the unit and say, "Breathe!" Reeve would be left struggling for air until he took a breath on his own.

At first, Reeve averaged only eighty cubic centimeters of air per breath, an amount that "wouldn't keep a parakeet alive," he explained.[7] There were days when he did not improve the numbers and days when he felt motivated to work harder. Gradually he made progress, up to 560 cubic centimeters per breath, freeing himself of the ventilator for hours at a time. Immediately after the accident, Reeve had been able to move only his head. Eventually, he was able to shrug his shoulders slightly.

Each day, Dana drove the eighty-five miles from their home in New York to the Kessler rehabilitation center in New Jersey, often in time to feed her husband his breakfast. "My main aide, Glen Miller, would always say when [Dana] walked into the room, 'Here comes your medication,'" Reeve remembered.[8] Even though he could not feel her touch, she held his hands and often sang him a song the two of them had sung to Will as a baby, "This Pretty Planet," by Tom Chapin.

Dana set up pictures of the family during happy times for Reeve to look at. She hung a poster with a picture of the space shuttle blasting off, autographed by astronauts at NASA, with the heading "We found nothing is impossible."[9]

"I would not be where I am today with the positive outlook that I have and the sense of real hope and purpose," Reeve said, "if it were not for Dana."[10]

Dana is the first to object to people's praise of her active role in her husband's rehabilitation. "I am not a saint," she said in an interview. She explained that, as in any of life's overwhelming challenges, she merely reacted to the situation and was glad that she did so in an honorable manner. "I've always felt uncomfortable with being [called] brave or whatever. It wasn't intentional."[11]

*After his surgery, Reeve had to adjust to life as a paraplegic. Here at the Kessler Institute for Rehabilitation in West Orange, New Jersey, he drew on his athletic background and began pushing himself to the limit. Just learning to breathe on his own for a few minutes at a time was a major challenge.*

"The thing that is hardest, I think," Dana said, "is for me to think about him playing the piano, because that's something not many people know that he knows how to do, and that's something that he and Will shared a lot."[12]

The wheelchair Reeve uses is a high-tech model that allows him to use his breath to control its movements. Black straps hold his hands on armrests, and a seat belt keeps him firmly in the chair. He either sips or puffs air into a tube, causing the chair to turn right or left and controlling its speed. His friend Robin Williams joked about the contraption: "He's afraid if he sneezes, he's gonna pop a wheelie and fly out the window!"[13]

All this care is not cheap. Reeve needs care twenty-four hours a day, and his medical bills total $400,000 a year. Because he had saved money from his acting roles, he was able to get the help he needed, but Reeve knew that most patients do not have that luxury. Many use up their insurance benefits, then sell off everything they own until they are living in poverty. Then they can qualify for Medicaid.

Reeve heard about a woman who was dependent on a ventilator and living at home. The vent tube became disconnected and she suffocated. When her family tried to recover damages in a lawsuit, the defense lawyer argued that the woman had "no quality of life anyway."[14] Reeve felt this was an unacceptable point of view. "The problem has been people have thought it was impossible [to do] anything for someone with . . . spinal cord injury," Reeve said. "That is simply false."[15] He decided to speak out, using his celebrity status once again to help others. "This insurance fight is . . . for the people down the hall from me at Kessler who are desperate and became my friends over the seven months I was there," he said later.[16]

Reeve also wanted to help himself. He knew that a complete recovery was generally considered impossible by the medical community, but even a small feat such as regaining the use of an arm would depend on major advances in spinal cord research. This, too, would require a lot of money.

Reeve was well prepared to lead the charge on spinal cord research. During all his previous work as an activist for the environment and the arts, he had met many people who could help him in a new cause—spinal cord research.

On September 29, 1995, Reeve made his first public appearance since the accident less than four months before. In a television interview with Barbara Walters, he described his condition to the viewers: "You become very knowledgeable about your body because you have lung problems, skin problems, bowel problems, bladder problems, all caused by the spinal cord. The brain can't get messages through to control these things."[17] He ended the interview, and many others, by saying that on his fiftieth birthday, he would like to stand and raise a glass to all who helped him. That was only seven years away.

Since Reeve knew that medical research is not always an exciting subject, he decided to use his own situation to appeal to people's hearts. He wanted people to see how medical research could truly change one's life. He made more television appearances, including an interview with Katie Couric on the *Today* show and one with Larry King on CNN's *Larry King Live*. He talked about the clock ticking closer and closer to his fiftieth birthday.

In October, Reeve felt ready to appear in public. The Creative Coalition was to have its annual Spotlight Award dinner in New York City, with one of the awards going to his good friend Robin Williams. As his wheelchair was rolled onto the stage, Reeve beamed his famous smile. The entire audience, filled with many of his close friends, stood, applauded, and cheered for a full five minutes. Some people wiped tears from their eyes.

Reeve spoke to the crowd, opening with a joke about the potholes on the city streets. That was the only reference he made to the extensive arrangements involved in getting him to the event. He did not mention what a huge operation it was for him to travel. For this event, it was worth all the effort.

Dana took care of most of the arrangements. She called ahead to make sure there was wheelchair access. She scheduled nurses so that one was always by her husband's side to monitor his blood pressure, make sure the ventilator was connected, and attend to his needs.

As the cheering crowd applauded, those difficulties were temporarily forgotten. Reeve spoke, telling the audience that he felt spinal cord research was close to a cure. Williams joked with him onstage, referring to his ventilator tube as a "nice tie." He told his friend, "You're on a roll, bro." With a nod toward Reeve's wheelchair, he added, "Literally."[18]

On December 13, 1995, Reeve was finally released from Kessler and allowed to go home. As he and Dana rode up the long driveway, their first look at the Bedford, New York, farmhouse was very emotional. It was wonderful to be back in familiar surroundings, but at the same time they realized that everything would be different. Even though he was home, it would never be the same. "Dana and I just sat in the driveway and held each other until I could sort of pull it together."[19]

The farmhouse had been remodeled, with ramps added and doorways widened to accommodate Reeve's wheelchair. Here in his old environment, Reeve could have experienced a serious depression, remembering all that he used to be able to do. Instead, being at home had the opposite effect on him. After only a few days, he was showing improvements in his breathing, blood pressure, oxygen levels, and blood count.

Reeve's therapy includes workout sessions to keep his muscles toned. Nurses exercise his limbs. They stretch his arms and legs for a warm-up, then move them strenuously to build up his muscles. Sometimes he wears special exercise shorts with electrodes that send electric currents to move his muscles. Reeve wants to keep his muscles in shape so his body will be ready when there is a cure for his injury.

While exercising, Reeve can look out the window to see the view. Goats and sheep run around the yard. White fencing surrounds green grass, with rolling hills in the distance beyond. "That's something I've learned to do since the injury—to look at things for long periods of time," he said.[20]

Those are peaceful times. However, there are frustrating times as well. Being paralyzed means Reeve is unable to do something as small as scratch an itch or brush away a stray hair. "I feel I'm always imposing," he said. "The more I can do for myself, the better I feel."[21]

But there is much that Reeve simply cannot do for himself, and he must struggle with life in a body he can scarcely move. He has no control over his bladder and cannot feed himself. When he is on the ventilator, the tube must be cleared from time to time, and Reeve's body must be shifted every couple of hours to keep his muscles flexible.

Reeve's relationship with his young son helps his state of mind. Will may run into the room and jump right onto his dad's lap. "He uses me as a jungle gym," Reeve said. "It would have been distressing if he had been afraid of me because I'm in a wheelchair."[22]

Just as distressing would be looks of pity from friends. "People visit and I sense them throwing glances around, being uncomfortable and uncertain," Reeve said. "But within moments, I can see them relax . . . anxiety, fear, or awkwardness fades away almost immediately."[23]

He knew it would help others to see him active again. Though stifled in a body unable to move, the old Christopher Reeve was back.

# A New Role

$C$hristopher Reeve's public life began picking up the pace once again. There would not be much time for staring out that picture window.

Joan Irvine Smith, a wealthy woman from California, had been horrified at Reeve's tragic accident, and she was especially touched that he never blamed his horse.[1] She contacted Reeve to let him know she had decided to help his cause by donating $1 million to establish the Reeve-Irvine Research Center, a facility dedicated to spinal cord research. She also set up a $50,000 prize for the neuroscientist who makes the most progress each year toward the goal of finding a cure for spinal cord injuries.

Reeve was also elected to the board of directors of the American Paralysis Association, another organization seeking a cure for spinal cord injuries. In the group's behalf, he received a pledge of $10 million in government funding from President Clinton.

There has been some controversy among the disabled regarding Reeve's insistence on a cure. Many disabled people feel that they should be accepted as they are. "When you say you want to cure me, you're saying there's something wrong with me," said one disability rights activist.[2]

Reeve's response is that the disabled should "realize they are entitled to much more out of life."[3] Reeve knows about life without disability. It is his life *before* the accident that he remembers well. "At night I am always whole," he said. "I've never had a dream in which I am in a wheelchair."[4]

Reeve was determined to live his life to the fullest. Going to the Academy Awards ceremony in Los Angeles would be an even bigger feat than going to the Creative Coalition dinner in New York City. Would it be possible for him to attend?

Again, this would be a live event, not taped. The producers would not be able to edit out anything unpleasant before the show aired on national television. Reeve was afraid that while he was onstage his arms or legs might go into violent spasms, which happens every now and then. His doctor tried to ease his fears. "If you spasm it's only human—it'll make people aware of what can happen to spinal cord victims."[5] But Reeve was worried that it would only make people feel sorry for him.

Luckily, everything went as planned at the Academy Awards. Toward the end of the telecast,

Christopher Reeve was introduced. His appearance was a surprise to almost everyone there, and, as at the Creative Coalition dinner, he received long, heart-felt applause. He opened with a joke. "What you don't know is that I left New York last September," he said, this time hinting at the difficulties surrounding his travel. "I just arrived here this morning."[6]

Later, Mel Gibson, who had won two Oscars for *Braveheart* that evening, proclaimed, "The attitude he's got—he'll walk. I have no doubts about it!"[7]

Reeve was beginning to convince many that this would be true. He made another appearance on CNN's *Larry King Live*, this time asserting, "I am going to get out of this chair, throw it away and walk."[8]

Reeve had been encouraged by the recent news from a spinal cord research center in Sweden. Researchers there had successfully transplanted nerves into rats with severed spines, and the injured nerves had then regenerated. As Dr. Wise Young explained, "The rats walked!"[9] Reeve's response when he heard the exciting news was, "Oh, to be a rat!"[10]

Being able to walk again was not Reeve's only concern. Another important issue was medical insurance. Insurance companies set a lifetime limit on how much they will pay for any one person's medical bills. Reeve's limit, for example, would be used up in only a few years. Most people who suffer from spinal cord injuries are not as financially well off as a celebrity like Reeve, and he knew the issue could be considered life-or-death to those who had run out of benefits.

Reeve paired up with his old friend Senator James Jeffords of Vermont. Reeve had supported Senator

Jeffords in environmental causes, and the senator now asked for Reeve's help on the insurance issue. Jeffords proposed a bill that would ban insurance companies from setting lifetime caps of less than $10 million. Most insurance companies will pay for medical costs up to a certain limit, often up to only $1 million. This is not nearly enough for those with serious injuries that require round-the-clock medical care. "[Reeve] was determined to help," said the senator. "He realizes what the caps do to thousands of others in this situation."[11]

Reeve's appearance on Capitol Hill hit home. "We know him as Superman, flying through the air," said Pennsylvania's Senator Arlen Specter. "To see him come in, propped up in a wheelchair, is really heart-breaking."[12]

Reeve began going on more outings with his family, even attending a New York Rangers hockey game. In the summer of 1996, he returned to one of his favorite sports, sailing in Shake-A-Leg's Wall Street Challenge Cup off Newport, Rhode Island. Reeve was once again able to feel the sense of freedom he used to enjoy when sailing out on the open sea. He breathed in the salty air and enjoyed the exhilarating speed as the boat cut across the water. "The more I do, the more I can do," Reeve said. "Sitting around doing nothing, and sleeping, do not agree with me."[13]

Dana agrees. Her life, too, has changed. Though she had also been a competitive horseback rider, she gave that up because she knew how much her husband would miss not being able to ride along with her. They had done so many activities together, but now they relish their private moments when small caresses mean so much. "A terrible thing happened. I wish it hadn't," Dana said. "But would it change who I married? Never."[14]

Reeve's older children, Matthew and Alexandra, visit as often as they can. Technology has helped them communicate with their father even when they are at their home in London. Reeve is unable to hold a telephone, but by using a computer program that recognizes his voice, he can talk to them between visits. This voice-activated program also enables him to explore the Internet, send e-mail, and even play chess with Matthew.[15]

Reeve acknowledges that this is very different from his days spent in strenuous athletics, but he looks at it positively. He had once been an active hockey player but now enjoys the sport by studying hockey team standings in the newspaper with Will. When Dana and Will play floor hockey in the house, Will pushes his dad's wheelchair to act as the Zamboni machine that cleans the ice. "While the activities have changed, there's a whole world for the heart, mind and spirit," Reeve said.[16]

Reeve has slowly resumed many things he had enjoyed before the accident, but some reports in the media have exaggerated his activities. One magazine reported that Reeve planned to fly a plane with controls that were operated like those on his wheelchair—by blowing through a tube. Reeve scoffed at those reports, saying they were "absolute Looney Tunes."[17]

Reeve's actual activities, however, do include making movies. He lent his voice for the part of King

Arthur in the animated movie *The Quest for Camelot*. He also directed an HBO original movie, *In the Gloaming* starring Glenn Close (*101 Dalmatians*) and Whoopi Goldberg (*Ghost*).

"I really wanted to be with Chris during his first directing experience," Glenn Close explained. "I've always been impressed with his dedication to and passion for the craft of acting, and I always thought those qualities would make him a wonderful director."[18]

Goldberg agreed. "Chris asked if I would mind taking a small part in the film. My immediate reaction was 'yes.'"[19]

The movie is about a man who is dying of AIDS. "[He] has to relate to his family, and they to him, in a different way, so that the ailment doesn't define him," explained Colin Callender, the executive vice president of HBO NYC Productions, which produced the movie. Reeve may have felt close to the story because it was similar to his own experience. "Chris had to redefine himself after his accident, and his family and friends had to redefine the way they relate to him," Callender said.[20]

The Reeve family seems to be doing fine in this new relationship. Reeve's son Will made an appearance in the movie, and Dana recorded the title song. They often visited the director on the set.

For this project, Reeve would later be nominated for an Emmy award in the category of Outstanding Director for a Miniseries or Special. Though he did not win, the HBO documentary he narrated, *Without Pity: A Film About Abilities*, won for Outstanding Informational Special. This show profiled many

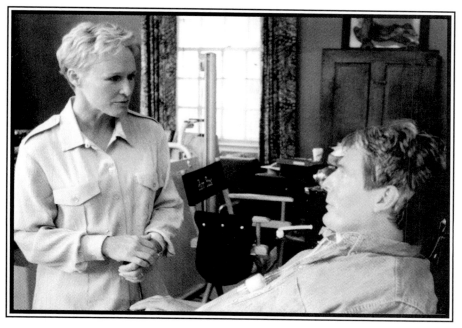

*After his accident, actor Christopher Reeve moved behind the camera to direct his first movie,* In the Gloaming, *starring Glenn Close (left) for HBO.*

different disabled people whose family and friends are helping them in their struggle to regain control of their lives.

The year 1997 was filled with many other awards as well. In January, Reeve was listed among *Good Housekeeping*'s top ten "Men We Admire Most." The reason? "Instead of letting tragedy turn him into a martyr, he became a true crusader," wrote one magazine subscriber who voted for Reeve.[21] Dana was also listed in the "Women We Admire Most" category, with another reader writing that "she exemplifies what marriage vows should mean. Her loyalty, courage and love are absolutely outstanding."[22]

In April, Reeve was honored with a star embedded in the sidewalk of Hollywood's Walk of Fame in Hollywood, California. Later in the year, Reeve was presented with a citation for courage at *GQ* magazine's annual Men of the Year Awards.

In his acceptance of these awards, Reeve remained humble. "I've seen people who are disabled, who have lost their insurance, who have lost their livelihood, who can't get the equipment they need, and yet they keep going," he said onstage at the *GQ* awards ceremony. "And by comparison my life is a piece of cake."[23]

He does not agree with those who say his injury was "meant to be," that it had another purpose. "It was an accident," he told a magazine reporter. "I believe it's what you do *after* a disaster that gives it meaning."[24]

Even so, Reeve's daily life has been a challenge. He has admitted that he allows himself time to cry in the mornings, then forces himself to move on.[25] In the years since his accident he has suffered from pneumonia a few times, two blood clots, a collapsed lung, and a broken arm.[26] He still endures occasional spasms, but they are normal for a quadriplegic. His bright blue eyes are as intense as ever, though he is still unable to move his body from his shoulders down. He sits strapped in his padded wheelchair, with an occasional whoosh coming from the ventilator as it supplies him with breath.

"Whether you're an adult who's been in a catastrophic accident or a child born with a disability,"

Reeve said, "there is really only one choice—and that is to go on."[27] Reeve's daily routine begins with ranging, a process by which his staff move his arms and legs to prevent muscle atrophy from lack of use. After about an hour of exercising, Reeve is given a sponge bath. Next, the bandages around his neck hole for the ventilator are changed, as are those around the catheter that drains his bladder. Finally, Reeve will be dressed and ready to begin the day—after up to three hours of preparations.[28]

*Christopher Reeve and his wife, Dana, at a 1997 concert in his honor in Princeton, New Jersey. Reeve visited his hometown to raise money for research to cure spinal cord injuries.*

Even with this extensive routine, Reeve found a way to return to his lifelong love—acting. He was executive producer and starred in the remake of Alfred Hitchcock's thriller *Rear Window*. Changes were made to accommodate the wheelchair-bound actor: Instead of suffering a mere broken leg, the character Reeve plays is paralyzed from the neck down. The stage set was all wheelchair accessible.

When not acting, Reeve is a forceful activist for spinal cord research, holding fund-raisers and giving speeches. "I'm president of a club I wouldn't have wanted to join," Reeve said, "but I'm grateful I can make a difference."[29]

On March 1, 1998, the television special *Christopher Reeve: A Celebration of Hope* aired on ABC, with many of his friends appearing onstage to offer their support. Robin Williams opened the fund-raising show by stating its purpose: "Basically, we're here to help my friend and 250,000 people get back on their feet again."[30] One of Reeve's childhood friends, the country singer Mary Chapin Carpenter, and other singers, including Stevie Wonder, Gloria Estefan, Amy Grant, Willie Nelson, and Aaron Neville, lent their voices to inspirational songs. Dana Reeve sang "The Music That Makes Me Dance." "It's special for us," she said, explaining her selection. "It's the song I sang the night Chris and I met."[31]

Christopher Reeve sat in the audience and smiled appreciatively. At the close of the show, he appeared onstage to speak to others with spinal cord injuries. "Help is on the way. Life will be better," he said in a raspy voice irritated by laryngitis. "We can hope, based on the dedication of millions of Americans who care about us."[32] The show raised $257,000.

And millions of people do care. Since his accident, Reeve has received more than four hundred thousand letters from people all over the world. One was from Steven Jurasits, who had broken his neck diving into shallow water. "I grew up watching you on the silver screen. You were my childhood idol," he wrote. "I now see you as a real-life idol and I hope I can feed off your aggressiveness to defeat this injury. Don't give up."[33]

Reeve knows his family, friends, and fans will not let him give up. When they tell him he is the real Superman, he knows they mean it.

"The fact that I [am] in a wheelchair, unable to move below my shoulders, and dependent on the support of others for almost every aspect of my daily life," Reeve said, "[has] not diminished the fact that I was— and always would be—their Superman."[34]

Reeve has shown the world what it means to be a true hero.

# Chronology

1952— Christopher Reeve is born in New York City on September 25.

1956— Reeve's parents divorce.

1968— Reeve works as an apprentice at the Williamstown Theatre Festival.

1970— Enrolls at Cornell University.

1973— Attends the Juilliard School for one year.

1974— Graduates from Cornell with a bachelor of arts in English; lands first television role on the soap opera *Love of Life*.

1976— Reeve's Broadway debut in *A Matter of Gravity* with Katharine Hepburn.

1977— Auditions for the role of Superman.

1978— *Superman* movie is released.

1979— Son Matthew is born to Christopher Reeve and Gae Exton.

1981— *Superman II* movie is released.

1983— *Superman III* is released; daughter Alexandra is born.

1987— Meets Dana Morosini in Williamstown; leads a rally in Chile in support of Amnesty International to prevent the execution of Chilean actors and directors.

1989— Helps found the Creative Coalition, with Susan Sarandon and other celebrities, to support the arts, the homeless, the environment, and other causes.

1990— Narrates a documentary for the Discovery Channel, *Black Tide*, about the tanker *Exxon Valdez* oil spill; speaks in Washington, D.C., in favor of the Clean Air Act.

1992— Marries Dana Morosini; son Will is born; campaigns for Democrats Bill Clinton and Al Gore for president and vice president.

1995— On May 27, suffers a broken neck in a riding accident that leaves him paralyzed.

1996— Attends the Academy Awards in Los Angeles; appears on Capitol Hill in Washington, D.C., to testify for increased lifetime insurance benefits.

1997— Receives an Emmy nomination for his direction of the HBO movie *In the Gloaming*; successfully testifies before the Senate for increased funding for spinal cord research by the National Institutes of Health.

1998— *Christopher Reeve: A Celebration of Hope* is aired as a fund-raiser for spinal cord research; publishes best-selling autobiography, *Still Me*; executive producer and star of a remake of Alfred Hitchcock's *Rear Window* on ABC-TV.

# Christopher Reeve Performs

## Selected Filmography

*Gray Lady Down*, 1978
*Superman: The Movie*, 1978
*Somewhere in Time*, 1980
*Superman II*, 1981
*Deathtrap*, 1982
*Monsignor*, 1982
*Superman III*, 1983
*The Bostonians*, 1984
*The Aviator*, 1985
*Street Smart*, 1987
*Superman IV: The Quest for Peace*, 1987
*Switching Channels*, 1988
*Noises Off*, 1992
*Morning Glory*, 1993
*The Remains of the Day*, 1993
*Speechless*, 1994
*Village of the Damned*, 1995

## Television

*Love of Life*, 1974–1976
*The Muppet Show*, 1981
*Faerie Tale Theater*, 1983
*Anna Karenina*, 1985
*The Great Escape: The Untold Story*, 1988

*Mortal Sins,* 1992
*The Sea Wolf,* 1993
*Above Suspicion,* 1995
*Black Fox,* 1995
*Without Pity: A Film About Abilities,* 1996 (narrator)
*In the Gloaming,* 1997 (director)
*Rear Window,* 1998

## Theater

*A Matter of Gravity,* 1976
*My Life,* 1977
*Fifth of July,* 1980
*The Greeks,* 1981
*The Aspern Papers,* 1984
*The Winter's Tale,* 1989
*Love Letters,* 1990
*The Guardsman,* 1992

# Chapter Notes

## Chapter 1. Up, Up and Away!

1. Kristin McMurran, "It's Stardom, Not Flying, That Christopher Reeve Fears: The Last Superman Shot Himself," *People*, January 8, 1979, p. 61.

2. Linda E. Watson, "A Down-to-Earth Actor . . . A Soaring Superstar," *Teen*, June 1983, p. 53.

3. Richard Collins, "People Who Fly—Christopher Reeve. Lights, Camera, Airplane," *Flying*, March 1981, p. 63.

4. Adrian Havill, *Man of Steel: The Career and Courage of Christopher Reeve* (New York: Penguin Books USA, 1996), p. 60.

5. Ibid., p. 66.

6. McMurran, p. 59.

7. Ibid.

8. Havill, p. 68.

9. McMurran, p. 59.

10. Havill, p. 68.

11. McMurran, p. 59.

12. Bruce Cook, "'Street Smart' Superman Up and Awry," *Los Angeles Daily News*, March 20, 1987, p. E9.

13. Christopher Reeve, *Still Me* (New York: Random House, 1998), p. 195.

14. Havill, p. 70.

15. Michael J. Bandler, "It Isn't Easy Being Superman!" *McCall's*, September 1987, p. 53.

16. Ibid., p. 54.

17. Reeve, p. 273.

18. Ibid.

## Chapter 2. "Being Somebody Else"

1. Sara Matthiessen, *After Dark*, October 1980, p. 50.

2. Karen S. Schneider, "Local Hero," *People*, January 27, 1997, p. 84.

3. Adrian Havill, *Man of Steel: The Career and Courage of Christopher Reeve* (New York: Penguin Books USA, 1996), p. 43.

4. Richard Collins, "People Who Fly—Christopher Reeve. Lights, Camera, Airplane," *Flying*, March 1981, p. 68.

5. Havill, p. 45.

6. Kristin McMurran, "It's Stardom, Not Flying, That Christopher Reeve Fears: The Last Superman Shot Himself," *People*, January 8, 1979, p. 61.

7. Bruce Cook, "'Street Smart' Superman Up and Awry," *Los Angeles Daily News*, March 20, 1987, p. E9.

8. Darryl Geddes, "Actor Reeve Urges Students to Embrace Love of Language," *Cornell Chronicle*, November 18, 1993.

9. "Christopher Reeve to Visit Campus," *Cornell Chronicle*, November 11, 1983.

10. Havill, p. 48.

11. Linda E. Watson, "A Down-to-Earth Actor . . . A Soaring Superstar," *'Teen*, June 1983, p. 52.

12. *Cornell Chronicle*, November 11, 1983.

13. Carol Tavris, "Christopher Reeve—A Superman Who's Only Human," *Mademoiselle*, October 1980, p. 84.

14. Christopher Reeve, *Still Me* (New York: Random House, 1998), p. 174.

15. Tavris, p. 72.

16. Watson, p. 52.

17. Ibid., p. 53.

18. Collins, p. 63.

19. Jack Kroll, "Superman to the Rescue!" *Newsweek*, January 1, 1979, p. 49.

20. Charles Michener, "Comedy of Bad Manners," *Newsweek*, February 16, 1976, p. 77.

21. "Christopher Reeve," *Biography Today 1997 Annual Cumulation* (Detroit: Omnigraphics, Inc., 1998), p. 248.

22. Peter Travers, "Chris Reeve Is 'Superman' and Super Dad—'Ear, 'Ear," *People*, July 6, 1981, p. 84.

## Chapter 3. Superman

1. Adrian Havill, *Man of Steel: The Career and Courage of Christopher Reeve* (New York: Penguin Books USA, 1996), p. 69.

2. Ibid.

3. Kristin McMurran, "It's Stardom, Not Flying, That Christopher Reeve Fears: The Last Superman Shot Himself," *People*, January 8, 1979, p. 61.

4. Jim Steranko, *The Steranko History of Comics* (New York: Crown, 1970), vol. 1, p. 38.

5. Nathan Aaseng, *The Unsung Heroes: Unheralded People Who Invented Famous Products* (Minneapolis, Minn.: Lerner Publications, 1988), pp. 53–57.

6. Reinhold Reitberger and Wolfgang Fuchs, *Comics: Anatomy of a Mass Medium* (Boston: Little, Brown and Company, 1971), p. 117.

7. Havill, p. 69.

8. McMurran, p. 59.

9. Ibid.

10. Linda E. Watson, "A Down-to-Earth Actor . . . A Soaring Superstar," *'Teen*, June 1983, p. 52.

11. McMurran, p. 59.

12. Jack Kroll, "Superman to the Rescue!" *Newsweek*, January 1, 1979, p. 51.

13. McMurran, p. 59.

14. Ibid., p. 61.

15. Richard Collins, "People Who Fly—Christopher Reeve, Lights, Camera, Airplane," *Flying*, March 1981, p. 63.

16. Carol Tavris, "Christopher Reeve—A Superman Who's Only Human," *Mademoiselle*, October 1980, p. 72.

17. Peter Travers, "Chris Reeve Is 'Superman' and Super Dad—'Ear, 'Ear," *People*, July 6, 1981, pp. 83–84.

## Chapter 4. A Star on the Subway

1. Jack Kroll, "Superman to the Rescue!" *Newsweek*, January 1, 1979, p. 49.

2. Pauline Kael, "The Package," *New Yorker*, January 1, 1979, p. 54.

3. Kroll, p. 51.

4. Kristin McMurran, "It's Stardom, Not Flying, That Christopher Reeve Fears: The Last Superman Shot Himself," *People*, January 8, 1979, p. 60.

5. Ibid., p. 61.

6. Aljean Harmetz, "On Location with Christopher Reeve," *The New York Times*, July 6, 1979, p. C5.

7. Adrian Havill, *Man of Steel: The Career and Courage of Christopher Reeve* (New York: Penguin Books USA, 1996), p. 100.

8. Ibid.

9. Ibid., p. 106.

10. Carol Tavris, "Christopher Reeve—A Superman Who's Only Human," *Mademoiselle*, October 1980, p. 84.

11. Peter Travers, "Chris Reeve Is 'Superman' and Super Dad—'Ear, 'Ear," *People*, July 6, 1981, p. 82.

12. Michael J. Bandler, "It Isn't Easy Being Superman!" *McCall's*, September 1987, p. 54.

13. Havill, p. 111.

## Chapter 5. Escape From the Cape

1. Richard Collins, "People Who Fly—Christopher Reeve. Lights, Camera, Airplane," *Flying*, March 1981, p. 64.

2. Ibid.

3. Ibid., p. 68.

4. Peter Travers, "Chris Reeve Is 'Superman' and Super Dad—'Ear, 'Ear," *People*, July 6, 1981, p. 84.

5. Sheila Benson, "'Superman II': A Human Touch to the Invincible," *Los Angeles Times*, January 18, 1981, calendar, part 6, p. 3.

6. Jack Kroll, "The Borgias Would Blanch," *Newsweek*, November 4, 1982, p. 90.

7. Adrian Havill, *Man of Steel: The Career and Courage of Christopher Reeve* (New York: Penguin Books USA, 1996), p. 136.

8. "Christopher Reeve," *Biography Today 1997 Annual Cumulation* (Detroit: Omnigraphics, Inc., 1998), p. 250.

9. Michael Burkett, "Flying High," *Santa Ana Orange County Register*, March 22, 1987, p. E12.

10. Havill, p. 148.

## Chapter 6. "Make a Difference"

1. Adrian Havill, *Man of Steel: The Career and Courage of Christopher Reeve* (New York: Penguin Books USA, 1996), p. 163.

2. Kathy Larkin, "Christopher Reeve Hit the Streets to Research Role," *Las Vegas Review Journal*, March 16, 1987.

3. Michael Burkett, "Flying High," *Santa Ana Orange County Register*, March 22, 1987, p. E12.

4. Jami Bernard, "Man of Steel's Life on the Street," *New York Post*, March 26, 1987, p. F3.

5. Darryl Geddes, "Actor Reeve Urges Students to Embrace Love of Language," *Cornell Chronicle*, November 18, 1993.

6. Michael J. Bandler, "It Isn't Easy Being Superman!" *McCall's*, September 1987, p. 54.

7. Havill, p. 181.

8. Joanna Powell, "Woman of Steel," *Good Housekeeping*, August 1997, p. 140.

9. Jeannie Park, "Eat Your Heart Out, Lois," *People*, April 20, 1992, p. 142.

10. Gregory Cerio, "Fallen Rider," *People*, June 12, 1995, p. 95.

11. Powell, p. 140.

12. Cerio, p. 94.

13. Bandler, p. 53.

14. Havill, p. 183.

15. Elizabeth Mehren, "Reeve's Real-Life Human-Rights Role in Chile," *Los Angeles Times*, December 30, 1987, calendar, part 6, p. 2.

16. Havill, p. 185.

17. Mehren.

18. Havill, p. 189.

19. Mehren.

20. Ralph Martin, "Celebrities Should Stick to Acting," *Electric Times Union*, April 2, 1990, p. B2.

21. Sharon Gazin, "Just a Regular Guy Actor Continues Coal Plant Fight," *Electric Times Union*, April 27, 1990, p. B6.

22. Havill, p. 209.

23. Park, p. 141.

24. Ibid., p. 142.

## Chapter 7. "Superman Is Down"

1. Jeannie Park, "Eat Your Heart Out, Lois," *People*, April 20, 1992, p. 143.

2. Adrian Havill, *Man of Steel: The Career and Courage of Christopher Reeve* (New York: Penguin Books USA, 1996), p. 223.

3. Darryl Geddes, "Actor Reeve Urges Students to Embrace Love of Language," *Cornell Chronicle*, November 18, 1993.

4. Havill, p. 8.

5. Ibid., p. 10.

6. Kendall Hamilton with Alden Cohen, "A Tragic Fall for Superman," *Newsweek*, June 12, 1995, p. 43.

7. Gregory Cerio, "Fallen Rider," *People*, June 12, 1995, p. 95.

8. Liz Smith, "We Draw Strength From Each Other," *Good Housekeeping*, June 1996, p. 87.

9. Cerio, p. 93.

10. Ibid.

11. Havill, p. 13.

## Chapter 8.  A Sign of Hope

1. Christopher Reeve, *Still Me* (New York: Random House, 1998), p. 34.

2. Roger Rosenblatt, "New Hopes, New Dreams," *Time*, August 26, 1996, p. 40.

3. Reeve, p. 32.

4. "Friends Indeed," *People*, October 30, 1995, p. 56.

5. Bruce Bibby, "Birds of a Feather," *Premiere*, April 1996, p. 64.

6. *People*, October 30, 1995.

7. Press release, June 9, 1995, on the Internet at <http://www.dot.net.au/~younis/reeve/statements.html> (September 2, 1997).

8. "The Will to Live," *People*, June 26, 1995, p. 55.

9. Press release, June 9, 1995, on the Internet at <http://www.dot.net.au/~younis/reeve/statements.html> (September 2, 1997).

10. Rosenblatt, p. 42.

11. Ibid., p. 45.

12. *People*, June 26, 1995, p. 56.

13. University of Virginia discharge statements, June 29, 1995, on the Internet at <http://www.dot.net.au/~younis/reeve/statements.html> (September 2, 1997).

14. Ibid.

15. Karen S. Schneider and Jane Shapiro, *People*, January 27, 1997, p. 86.

16. Ibid.

17. Marny Smith, "Strokes of Strength," *Women's Sports & Fitness*, September 1996, p. 41.

18. Joanna Powell, "Woman of Steel," *Good Housekeeping*, August 1997, p. 100.

## Chapter 9.  "Nothing Is Impossible"

1. Christopher Reeve, *Still Me* (New York: Random House, 1998), p. 44.

2. Roger Rosenblatt, "New Hopes, New Dreams," *Time*, August 26, 1996, p. 46.

3. Ibid.

4. Reeve, p. 114.

5. Liz Smith, "We Draw Strength From Each Other," *Good Housekeeping*, June 1996, p. 89.

6. Adrian Havill, *Man of Steel: The Career and Courage of Christopher Reeve* (New York: Penguin Books USA), 1996, p. 241.

7. Smith, p. 89.

8. Claudia Perry, "Kessler Foundation Honors Dignity of Actors, Reeve, Vereen, *The Star-Ledger* (Newark, N.J.), September 27, 1998, sec. 1, p. 35.

9. Speech at the Democratic National Convention, August 26, 1996, on the Internet at <http://www.dot.net.au/~younis/reeve/statements.html> (September 2, 1997).

10. "The Journey of Christopher Reeve," *20/20*, ABC News, September 29, 1995, transcript, p. 6.

11. Joanna Powell, "Woman of Steel," *Good Housekeeping*, August 1997, p. 140.

12. "The Journey of Christopher Reeve," *20/20*, ABC News, September 29, 1995, transcript, p. 5.

13. Bruce Bibby, "Birds of a Feather," *Premiere*, April 1996, p. 64.

14. *The Oprah Winfrey Show*, ABC-TV, May 4, 1998, transcript, p. 9.

15. James Barron, "Christopher Reeve Backs a Registry," *The New York Times*, September 22, 1998, p. D2.

16. Trip Gabriel, "Will the Insurers Feel His Sting?" *The New York Times*, April 11, 1996, p. C8.

17. *20/20*, p. 3.

18. "Friends Indeed," *People*, October 30, 1995, p. 56.

19. Rosenblatt, p. 51.

20. Ibid., p. 49.

21. Ibid., p. 50.

22. Smith, p. 88.

23. Ibid.

## Chapter 10. A New Role

1. Roger Rosenblatt, "New Hopes, New Dreams," *Time*, August 26, 1996, p. 42.

2. Kendall Hamilton, "Fighting to Fund an 'Absolute Necessity,'" *Newsweek*, July 1, 1996, p. 56.

3. Ibid.

4. Dinitia Smith, "A Life With a Before and an After," *The New York Times*, April 30, 1998, p. E1.

5. Trip Gabriel, "Will the Insurers Feel His Sting?" *The New York Times*, April 11, 1996, p. C8.

6. *The Academy Awards Ceremony*, January 1996, ABC-TV, March 25, 1996.

7. Adrian Havill, *Man of Steel: The Career and Courage of Christopher Reeve* (New York: Penguin Books USA), 1996, p. 260.

8. *Larry King Live*, CNN, February 21, 1996.

9. Sharon Begley, "To Stand and Raise a Glass," *Newsweek*, July 1, 1996, p. 52.

10. Liz Smith, "Christopher Reeve Envies Laboratory Rats," *The Star-Ledger* (Newark, N.J.), October 20, 1997, p. 29.

11. Michelle Green, "He Will Not Be Broken," *People*, April 15, 1996, p. 125.

12. Hamilton, p. 56.

13. Lawrie Mifflin, "After a Life in Front of a Camera, a New One Behind It," *The New York Times*, October 31, 1996, p. C18.

14. Joanna Powell, "Woman of Steel," *Good Housekeeping*, August 1997, p. 141.

15. Liz Smith, "We Draw Strength From Each Other," *Good Housekeeping*, June 1996, p. 89.

16. *Today*, NBC-TV, October 17, 1997.

17. Marilyn Beck and Stacy Jenel Smith, "Reeve Clips Wings of Rumors About Flying Lessons," *The Star-Ledger* (Newark, N.J.), August 11, 1997, p. 27.

18. "Glenn Close, Bridget Fonda, Whoopi Goldberg, Robert Sean Leonard, and David Strathairn Star in the Intimate HBO Drama *In the Gloaming*; Christopher Reeve's Directorial Debut, Film Debuts April 20," press release from Home Box Office (HBO), March 19, 1997.

19. Ibid.

20. Mifflin, p. C18.

21. "The Women and Men We Admire Most," *Good Housekeeping*, January 1997, p. 122.

22. Ibid.

23. *GQ* Men of the Year Awards acceptance speech, Radio City Music Hall, New York City, October 15, 1997.

24. Rosenblatt, p. 48.

25. *48 Hours*, CBS-TV, May 15, 1997.

26. Joshua Harris Prager, "Superman Transforms Spinal Research," *Wall Street Journal*, November 18, 1998, p. B1.

27. Michael Overall, "Having Hope," *Tulsa World*, May 16, 1997.

28. Christopher Reeve, *Still Me* (New York: Random House, 1998), p. 264.

29. "A Life Redefined," *Life*, November 1998, p. 68.

30. *Christopher Reeve: A Celebration of Hope*, ABC-TV, March 1, 1998.

31. Sue Factor, "Reeve's Special Night Raises Hope," *USA Today*, February 3, 1998, p. 2D.

32. *Christopher Reeve: A Celebration of Hope*.

33. *The Oprah Winfrey Show*, May 4, 1998, transcript, p. 15.

34. Reeve, p. 194.

# Further Reading

Finn, Margaret L. *Christopher Reeve: Actor and Activist.* Boomall, Pa.: Chelsea House, 1997.

Havill, Adrian. *Man of Steel: The Career and Courage of Christopher Reeve.* New York: Penguin Books USA, 1996.

Hughes, Libby. *Christopher Reeve.* Parsippany, N.J.: Dillon Press, 1998.

Petrov, David. *The Making of Superman, the Movie.* Boston, Mass.: Warner Books, 1978.

Reeve, Christopher. *Still Me.* New York: Random House, 1998.

Rosenblatt, Roger. "New Hopes, New Dreams." *Time,* August 26, 1996.

• • • •

The Christopher Reeve Foundation
P.O. Box 277
FDR Station
New York, NY 10150-0277
888-711-HOPE
www.APACURE.com

## Internet Addresses

### Unofficial Christopher Reeve Homepage
<http://www.geocities.com/Hollywood/Studio/4071/>

### Celeb Site Profile: Christopher Reeve
<http://www.celebsite.com/people/christopherreeve/index.html>

# Index